War at Wind River

He came to Wind River with no memory – but with six notches carved into his Colt. And when three men tried to kill him only one got away alive – and even he was wounded.

The local sheriff didn't like the idea of a gunfighter in his town, even if the man didn't *know* he was a gunfighter. There were others who didn't want him there either – some didn't even want him *alive.*

There was only one thing he could do: find out who he really was. Even if it meant dodging bushwhackers' bullets. His one big fear was that maybe he wouldn't want to know even when he did learn the truth.

By the same author

Long-Riding Man
The Mustang Strip
Brazos Station
Hell's Doorway
Die Like a Man
Wait for Lobo
Missouri Avenger
Judgement Day at Yuma
Killer Instinct
Red River Riot
Run for the Money
Man from Blood Creek
Rio

War at Wind River

CLAYTON NASH

ROBERT HALE · LONDON

First published in Great Britain 2004

ISBN 0 7090 7618 5

Robert Hale Limited
Clerkenwell House
Clerkenwell Green
London EC1R 0HT

Typeset by
Derek Doyle & Associates, Liverpool.
Printed and bound in Great Britain by
Antony Rowe Limited, Wiltshire

CHAPTER 1

MAN OF MYSTERY

The second getaway horse died under him a couple of hours before sundown with three-quarters of the killer desert still to cross.

He felt it stagger and knew it must be that damn bushwhacker's bullet. Heading through Cowskull Pass, no reason to think he hadn't lost the posse or that there might be someone who had figured out his getaway trail and ridden on ahead to lie in wait. Then just that single shot – and although he had felt the horse kind of swerve, with a grunting sound, he hadn't realized it had been hit – it felt more like the bullet had punched into the saddle leather. Anyway, he was too intent on getting away to start working theories right then.

He had stretched out over the mount's neck, rowelling with the spurs, and with a snorting lunge the horse was away. It was an experienced cattle horse, responded instantly to the pressure of his knees and tugs on the reins, leaving the pass in a cloud of dust. If the bushwhacker wanted to try again he wouldn't have had a decent target to shoot at. If there was any more gunfire it was lost in the echoing drumbeat of hoofs as he burst out into open country.

He kept the mount going fast for half a mile before he slowed a little, sat up and half-hipped in leather to get a look at his back trail.

He smiled thinly: that feller had outsmarted himself. Found a good spot up on the rim above the trail through the pass, settled in, might even have had time to drive a forked stick into the ground so as to support the fore-end of the rifle, and then waited for him to show.

One shot, he must have figured on. Bring down the mount and man with one bullet, likely shifting aim downwards to prepare for his next shot as the rider sprawled and sat up dazedly beside the kicking horse.

Except the tough old cow pony had taken that bullet and kept right on going in response to the spurs.

Then the gunman had been unable to see clearly for any further shots because of the dust cloud – and his only option was to climb on down and follow on horseback if he wanted his quarry.

And that was where he had lost out. There was no trail that led directly down into the pass from up there. The desert side ended in sheer cliffs. So the rifleman would have to mount up, ride on back down the far side of the range and then find his way to the pass and come on through.

By that time, the fugitive would be long lost in the heat-haze of the badlands and the alkali was so fine out here it was like talc, dusted everything that passed over it in a dirty glaring white. It was fine enough to fill in the tracks of anything that walked on it, man or beast. Some said even a fly wouldn't leave tracks out here.

Which was one reason he had chosen this area for his escape.

But the horse had slowed and he knew he couldn't go any further without checking for a wound and treating it if necessary. The first getaway mount had busted a leg in the whitewater of that unnamed river three days ago. He had been lucky to pick up this tough old bag of rawhide from a round-up camp while the crew were busy passing around a couple of young Arapaho squaws they had likely come upon at the river, bathing or doing their laundry.

The bullet had gone in just under the rear of the saddle, luckily missing the spine, but glancing off a rib. And the lead was still in there. He placed his ear against the sweaty hide, held his breath – and heard the bubbling sounds.

Hell! Bleeding internally!

Well, he knew he wasn't going to make it across the badlands on this horse. He stared into the glare behind him. No signs of pursuit, but someone would be out there. Someone smart – for he had lost the posse days earlier. This loner must be a bounty hunter or a lawman who really took his job seriously.

He had a feeling the man was coming. He might not be able to see him, but his instincts told him he was back there – somewhere. And he wasn't finished with him yet.

So he had washed the wound, given the horse much more water than he could afford and mounted up again, hoping to make those distant dunes by sundown.

Now the horse was dead and had fallen on his warbag and rifle scabbard, leaving him with only his six-gun and knife as weapons – and no change of clothes from the rags he was wearing. The canteen sounded frighteningly hollow and there was ten miles between him and the dunes. And no water there, either, nothing but sand to the horizon, not a tree or a blade of grass to be seen.

But there was delirium – and death.

Behind, he likely wouldn't know fever and illusion, but death was there, for certain-sure. . . .

There was, of course, no choice.

So he tugged and wrenched at the bedroll but the warbag wouldn't come free, slung the too-light canteen across his chest, tossed the horse a brief salute by way of thanks and set out for the dunes.

The sun, even this late in the day, seemed to strike his shoulders through his ragged shirt like the physical blows of a bullwhip, repeated over and over and over, beating him down, sapping the very life out of him. . . .

He heard birds.

Couldn't be. But – there it was again! Bird calls, even the beating of wings and – just couldn't be! Not the trickling of water. . . !

He didn't know why such thoughts came into his head. They were just there – and gone again. Then he opened his eyes slowly and felt such a shock he actually thought his heart skipped a beat.

Greenery all round. A mountain stream setting basalt rocks glistening in bright sunlight. A blurred streak, several blurred streaks against the tall, waving tree tops – birds, all right. But what shocked him most was the shape that moved between him and those trees.

A head. A human head, surrounded by a halo of golden red and a soft voice asking, 'Are you feeling better, Mr Benbow?'

He couldn't answer. His tongue felt swollen in his mouth. He had a headache that made him wonder if his skull had been split in two by a stone tomahawk. One eye, his left, seemed to have something blocking its full vision, and it was sticky.

Then it hit him. *Benbow!*

That was what she had called him – but it wasn't familiar. Maybe she had him mixed up with someone else.

He was—

This time he was sure his heart did actually stop for a beat or two.

He couldn't remember! He didn't know who he was!

There was sundown colour smearing the sky when he came round again and he heard the soft crackling of flames. Turning his head, he saw the woman hunkering down, feeding kindling to an infant camp-fire. The sundown had turned her chestnut hair to an even deeper gold and her face was pale against this as she snapped her head around when he spoke in a gravelly voice, absently rubbing at a raw mark that almost encircled his right wrist, 'How did you know my name?'

She crossed to him swiftly, kneeling, and he noticed she wore denim trousers and a soft leather vest over a checked shirt. She seemed young, twenties, maybe. She smiled, reached out a hand to touch his hot forehead.

'Why, when I found you, you were unconscious from that head wound – I felt justified in going through your jacket pockets. There's a letter in there, addressed to "Mr Al Benbow, General Delivery, Laramie" – it was from someone named "Kip" – I have the impression he's your brother.'

The man frowned, trying to absorb this, his face going through a series of expressions ranging from worry to shock to something akin to fear and back to puzzlement.

Her hand squeezed his hand, and she casually noticed the raw mark on his wrist. Her smile widened. 'It's all right – I'm Tess Dalton. You're on my land just north of the Wind River. You're all right now.' But then the smile faded a little as she added, 'I say that a trifle uncertainly, because that wound in your head is a bullet wound. But I think it's a day or two old, so if someone was pursuing you, I'd say you may have given them the slip. Anyway, I've sent for a buckboard and we'll soon get you into town.'

'Which . . . town?'

'Why, Lander – that's the nearest town to here.'

Her frown deepened. 'You do know you're in Wyoming, don't you?'

He hesitated, then nodded, forcing a small smile. 'Sure – sure I do. . . . Tell me, you have deserts in Wyoming? *Real* deserts I mean – sand, alkali, dunes, salt lakes?'

Tess Dalton backed off a little. 'We have dry-grass plains that stretch for hundreds of miles, but no real deserts such as you described. Why d'you ask?'

There was a strange, wary tone in her voice now.

He licked his cracked lips. 'I . . dunno. I just had this impression of . . . something like hell. Red-hot sands, no trees, no water. . . .'

The smile returned and her small hand patted his gently. She noticed the wrist mark again, turned his hand to study it but said nothing, smiling at him. 'You were dreaming, likely had a touch of fever. Your clothes are covered in leaves and twigs and they look as if you have fallen in the river recently. The cloth's all wrinkled and a little muddy.' She laughed briefly. 'You're hundreds of miles from a desert of sand and alkali. Even that buckskin horse of yours shows no sign of having done any desert travel recently so just try to relax and we'll soon have you in to a doctor.'

Relax?

He felt terrible, like his head belonged to someone else, someone who had been kicked by a mule. His mind was aswirl with overlapping visions, part-dreams, impressions.

And each one scared the living daylights out of him.

He felt as if he was floating in limbo, nowhere to

go, no memory backwards, and only fear and the unknown ahead.

Relax?

He felt more like screaming.

Doc Gabriel wasn't an angel even if his name had conjured up such an image in Benbow's tortured mind. The sawbones was thick-bodied, medium tall, more like a man used to manual labour than a doctor. But he did have fine-fingered hands.

And now they probed gently at Benbow's wound as he sat on the edge of the narrow bed in Gabriel's small infirmary. 'Hurt – there?' the doctor asked, touching just below the wound on his left temple.

'Like – *hell*, Doc! Take it easy, will you?'

'I'm sorry but it's necessary. Here? Very well, don't cuss so much. Vision problems? Nausea? Headache I should imagine. . . ?'

'I got a hangover that belongs to five other fellers who've just cut loose their curly wolf.'

Gabriel managed a smile and his squarish face softened some. 'That I can well believe. You have concussion, my friend, and I suspect that your memory isn't what it should be. . . . Kind of mixed-up? Unclear?'

He was obviously waiting for some kind of reply and Benbow looked at him out of his reddened eyes, scratched at the full-blown beard that itched as if it was full of crawling things. But he had been bathed before the doctor had gone to work on the wound, which, Gabriel told him, was a shallow bullet burn – but it had slightly depressed the skull in one spot.

The spot his fingers had probed and which had almost made Benbow leap off the bed.

'Doc,' he said after a long silence. 'I . . . feel confused. Lots of crazy things cramming into my head – makes it ache worse. Feel like I'm falling all the time, want to grab at something to keep from dropping into some kind of hole – and it looks mighty black down there.'

'Lie down, Mr Benbow.' Gabriel exerted gentle pressure on his chest and pushed him back on the bed. 'You need to rest – and I'm sure you feel more steady lying still.'

He did and he squinted at the medico. 'You seem to know more about how I feel than I do myself, Doc.'

'I've had a little experience with wounds such as yours during the War. Where were you born, by the way?'

'In—' Benbow stopped dead, feeling the prickling of his skin as the fear washed over him. His hands gripped at the sheets, crumpling them. He stared hard at Gabriel. 'I – my mind's a blank, Doc! I – I can't remember!'

The doctor nodded. 'You have a name for your horse?'

Benbow merely stared.

'You look like a cowboy – which ranch did you last work for?'

'Christ! Ease up, Doc! You – you're scaring me white!' He noticed for the first time that he had a narrow bandage around his right wrist.

Gabriel had been pouring a dark medicine into a

glass from a brown bottle with ridges on one side. He lifted Benbow's head gently and held the glass to his lips. 'You have some kind of injury on your wrist. Healing, but I've put ointment on it and wrapped it to avoid infection. Drink, please.'

'God, that tastes foul!'

Gabriel smiled as he lowered him back to the pillow. 'You'll feel drowsy soon . . . rest and sleep is what you need right now.'

Benbow groped for one of those fine-fingered hands, found it and gripped tightly. 'What the hell's wrong with me, Doc?'

'You have a form of amnesia. Temporary, I hope, but it does need treatment.'

'What is it? Is that the fancy name they use when a man loses his memory?'

'Exactly that, Mr Benbow.' Gabriel smiled again as he saw signs that the sleeping draught was taking effect. 'Look on the bright side, at least we know your name. That's the very best starting point.'

Benbow tried to answer him but the words were slurred and it was only as he was going out the door that the doctor realized what his patient had said.

'Leave . . . my . . . gun. . . .'

CHAPTER 2

'SOMEONE KNOWS YOU!'

'Thought you were supposed to've killed him!'

Hilton Granger moved no part of his body except his icy blue eyes as he stared across the room at the big man in soiled range garb who sat tensely on the edge of the straight-backed chair opposite him.

The man cleared his throat, turned his hat slowly between big hands now covered in worn and dirty chamois work gloves. The man was long-jawed, stubbled, and his tongue flickered into view as he licked his dry, wide lips. His nose was large, bent a little out of shape, and brown eyes were shadowed by heavy brows. Sweat plastered black hair flat to his bullet-shaped skull.

He spoke slowly and distinctly. 'I hit him in the head. Long ways south of here, down on Pike Flats. Him and the hoss went over the edge into the river.

When I got there, he had his hand caught in the reins, trailin' out to one side, the hoss rollin' in whitewater. Nothin' but rocks and rapids downstream. Boss, I put my field-glasses on him and he looked dead to me, blood all over his face, body bobbin' crazily, the damn buckskin pullin' him under more times than he was afloat – I went downstream later but couldn't see hide nor hair and there was only that big drop over Pike's Falls, so . . .'

Granger held up a hand, his cold gaze still making the big man squirm slightly. 'All right, Jethro. You did your best and I'll admit I'd've said he had to be dead, too.' Then one hand clenched into a fist and slammed on to the arm of the easy chair like a hammer blow. Jethro jumped as Granger leaned forward. 'But he *ain't* dead if you saw the Dalton woman takin' him into Doc Gabriel's!'

Jethro swallowed and shook his head. 'No, he ain't dead, boss. I know it was him – that damn buckskin and all, tied to the tailgate of Tess's buckboard.'

Granger continued to stare until Jethro stood awkwardly, unsure of what to say or do. 'Thought – thought I'd better let you know.'

'You've done that. So why're you still standin' here?'

Jethro frowned, drawing those beetling brows closer above his nose that cleaved the air like the bow of a ship. 'I – uh – what d'you want me to do, boss?'

'He's . . . still . . . alive. . . .' Granger glared, still frozen in that forward stance, as if he was about to lunge across the room.

Jethro's frown deepened. 'Judas! You mean—? *In*

town? Right on Heffernan's doorstep?'

'Finish the job, Jethro.'

'Christ, it's risky! I mean, we ain't even sure—'

Granger stood, average height, solidly built, an arrogant tilt to his head and a jaw that jutted aggressively. He spoke quietly. 'Could be more risky for you *not* to finish the job, Jethro . . . think about that. But do it outside, while you're saddlin' your horse.'

Jethro Caine nodded slowly, his tongue running across his dry lips again as he started for the ranch-house door. 'I'll wait till dark.'

'Do what you like. Report back to me when you're through. There's plenty of work to be done around this place, but I like one job completed before movin' on, savvy?'

Granger poured himself a whiskey at a battered sideboy standing against the wall of the parlour near a window that looked out over the ranch yard. He didn't offer Jethro any and the man didn't hesitate more than a second when he realized he wasn't going to get a drink.

Caine opened the door and hurried out, bawling at one of the roustabouts to saddle his horse for him, pronto. He was a new kid named Chuck and seemed to have taken a shine to Jethro. 'Anythin' you say, Jethro!' Chuck said, swaggering.

'The black,' Caine added, heading now for the bunkhouse to pick up his rifle. 'I want somethin' with speed and muscle . . . and tell Chance I want to see him.'

The roustabout waved casually, walking briskly enough towards the corral. Caine grinned crookedly.

His six-gun crashed and a bullet spurted gravel between the kid's boots. He threw a scared look at Caine standing with the smoking gun in his hand and started to run.

Jethro grinned: it gave him a kick to see people scared of him.

Tess Dalton called in to Doc Gabriel's after finishing some shopping in town.

As she went up on to the porch, the door opened and Sheriff Howie Heffernan came out. He glared at her, a rawboned, lanky man with a mournful face and a hard mouth. His eyes watered a lot because he was short of lashes and the lids always showed pink and damp. Fine red hair showed beneath his curl-brim hat.

'You could've come told me you brought in a man with a head wound, Tess,' he said irritably.

'I thought it more important to get him medical treatment, Howie. I was just going to find out from Doc how he's doing and then come and give you a full report.'

Heffernan sniffed, not moving his gaze. 'Doc says he's lost his memory. Because of that damn bullet wound. Somethin' like this happens in my bailiwick I need to know right away. You oughta know that.'

Tess sighed. 'I'm sorry, Howie. It all happened so fast and unexpectedly – I'll come down and make a written statement as soon as I talk to Doc.'

The sheriff refused to be mollified. He shouldered past her rudely, muttering, 'What you should've done in the first place. I'll be waitin'.'

Inside, Tess smiled slightly as Gabriel came across his waiting-room. 'Howie's crossing "i's" and dotting his "t's" again.'

Gabriel laughed shortly. 'He'll worry himself into an ulcer one of these days. If you've come to see our mystery man, he's sleeping. Gave him a draught of laudanum.'

Tess sobered. 'Is it true he's lost his memory?'

'Seems so. It's consistent with that head wound. Skull plate's just depressed enough to exert unwanted pressure on the brain.'

'Will he remember again?'

Gabriel hesitated and then made a shrugging motion. 'I can't say, Tess. But I – I have a radical method I might try. I'll see how he is when he wakes up.'

'Well, at least we know his name.'

'Circumstantial, but it's a place to start, I suppose.' At her puzzled frown he added, 'I mean we can't be certain that letter was his.'

'Why would he be carrying it if it wasn't? It read as if it was from his brother, asking for money because he was in trouble with gambling debts.'

Gabriel nodded a trifle impatiently. 'Yes, yes, I know. I was just looking at all possibilities. But for now, we won't disturb him, Tess. I'll let you know his progress if you want.'

'Ye-es – I'd like to know how he's going. I feel somewhat – involved.'

'I understand.'

She took her leave, frowning a little as she started back towards Main, remembering she had to make her statement to the sheriff.

She was sure the day could only improve after that.

He felt as if there was a tight band about his forehead, tied to a massive weight that was holding his head down, sunk deep into the pillow.

It was dark and there were few night sounds, although the place was fairly close to Main Street. *Must be late, or even the early hours of morning,* he thought but even that small effort brought a frown to his face and a squinting of his eyes. *God! I've never had a hangover like this before!*

He lay there, remembering where he was, remembering how he had come here in the back of a jolting buckboard – driven by – a woman! *Tess someone . . . Dawson? Dalton!*

The doctor had treated him for a – headwound. He put up his hand and felt gingerly at the pad of cotton taped above his left eye. *A bullet wound. . . .* That was what the doctor had said . . . *now how did I get that?*

There was an end to memory. Nothing beyond the half-dream of regaining consciousness near a river with birds singing in the trees and the girl bending over him – and the fast fading image of a hellish desert. She had told him his name was Benbow, Al Benbow. He couldn't argue with her although he had an uncomfortable feeling when that name was applied to him. Couldn't argue because he couldn't remember his name – or anything beyond that moment when he had first heard the song of the birds.

He felt his belly knotting and his hands clawed at the sheets as he lay there in the dark. Sweat beaded his body and trickled down his face. *No memory at all!*

He had never known such a grip of fear.

Then there was a shattering of glass to his right and despite the pain he snapped his head that way as the twin barrels of a shotgun came into view and even as he recognized them, a sheet of flame erupted and the room was filled with thunder.

He was on the floor on the left side of the bed, a cocking six-gun in his hand as he saw his mattress erupt into an explosion of feathers and fabric. Gunsmoke rasped harshly at his nostrils as he thumbed the hammer of his Colt and it bucked twice against his wrist. More glass shattered, a man grunted and reared up, struck the frame and tumbled forward over the sill. Someone cursed and a second man-shape appeared, six-gun in hand, blasting wildly into the room. Bullets thunked into the remains of the bed, ripped up one wall, tearing loose lathes and paper. A third clanged off a metal bowl, sending it spinning across the room.

Then Benbow's Colt roared again, three shots this time, and the man howled, spun away. There was a clatter and another curse, some sounds he couldn't identify until they transformed into the pounding of running boots.

He was dragging himself across the destroyed bed when the door burst open and Doc Gabriel charged in, a large Colt Dragoon pistol in his hand, his wife in her nightcap and clutching her gown tightly to her throat following timidly.

'Benbow! Are you all right?'

Gabriel rushed to the bed and Benbow turned to him and said he was all right, adding, 'There's a dead man under the window. . . .'

The doctor straightened. 'Good Lord!' He crouched as he approached the shattered window, voices outside now calling to know what was wrong. He turned slowly towards the exhausted man on the the bed.

'There are two dead men here, Benbow – one inside, one outside.'

The doctor crossed to the bedside table, straightened it and lit the lamp that smoked badly, after lying on its side – the oil had almost drowned the wick.

'The sheriff will be here shortly, dear,' he said calmly to his wife. 'Perhaps you had better dress . . . Benbow, I need to examine you after your – exertions.'

He seemed wary of the patient now as his wife hurried out. He held the Dragoon so that it more or less covered Benbow, who smiled wryly.

'Relax, Doc – no danger now. I think I heard a third man run off.'

'It seems that someone knows you after all.'

Benbow looked at him sharply as gawking townsmen crowded around the window, looking at the dead men.

Someone said, 'This here's that no-good 'breed they call Smoky.'

Another man, peering into the room at the dead man with the shotgun trapped beneath his body amongst the broken glass, said, 'And this here's that hardcase Chance from Circle G. . . . Him an' Smoky was s'posed to be kin I heard once.'

Sheriff Heffernan arrived in a sour mood, blinking his watery eyes, glowering around the room, pushing out the couple of inquisitive men who had climbed in the window to get a closer look at Benbow. He shouted at the gawkers to go back to their beds, then rounded on Benbow.

'Seems you're more than you let on, mister – beat a shotgun blast out of that bed and nailed the two sonuvers who tried to kill you.'

Benbow looked at the lawman without speaking for a long moment, then shrugged. 'Just did it, Sheriff. Don't recall giving it any thought. Saw the shotgun and next thing I know I'm shooting across the bed through a cloud of rags and feathers.'

'That kind of thing don't need to be thought about,' Heffernan said sourly. 'It's one of them things comes naturally to a certain kinda man – I think I need to look into you a lot deeper than I planned, Mr Al Benbow.'

'That's a good idea, Sheriff,' spoke up the doctor, standing beside Benbow who was sitting on the edge of the bed still, his Colt on the floor between his bare feet. 'I think this man needs to know his past somewhat urgently.'

'What's the hurry?' the sheriff growled. 'I'll find out who he is eventually. I got plenty of time.'

Gabriel gestured at the dead man lying under the window. 'There could be others where he came from. By the by, someone said he was Chance from Granger's spread. That might be a starting point, Howie.'

Heffernan didn't need anyone telling him how to do his job. 'You stick to your iodine and laxatives, Doc, let me handle any investigation into this feller. And you, Benbow, you stay put . . . unless Doc'll agree to me holdin' you in one of my cells. . . .'

'I damn well will not!' interjected Gabriel, outraged.

Heffernan waved a hand. 'Figured that – but I'm makin' you responsible for him, Doc. Until I find out more about this feller's past, he's what you might call under open arrest.'

Benbow lifted his head slowly, and nodded gently at the lawman. 'I'd like to know myself, Sheriff. Where you figure to start?'

Heffernan was about to bristle again but changed his mind and said curtly, 'That letter you got was adressed to Al Benbow, General Delivery, Laramie. Someone there likely knows you. And then there's Chance and that breed Smoky. He'd slit his mother's throat for the price of a drink and Chance has been in a heap of trouble in this town for brawlin' – I'm damn sure he kicked a man to death six months ago but could never prove it. He'd hire out for extra money. Granger might know somethin', seein' as Chance worked for him.'

'Who's this Granger?'

'Hell, man, he's the richest and biggest rancher hereabouts. And he'll be even richer and bigger when the railroad comes. Whole town will, for the matter of that. Hilt Granger runs the Circle G – you must've heard of that? No? Well, you really have lost your memory if you dunno about Circle G. But you just rest easy. I'll find out who you are. And why someone wants you dead.'

Well, that was obvious, of course, Benbow thought bitterly. *I turn up with a bullet wound in the head, and a couple of hired guns try to blow me to hell with a shotgun. Sooner I get my memory back the better, before someone snuffs it out for good.*

He had been holding the Colt, angled it up so he could punch out the used shells. Now he felt something rough along one edge of the butt. He didn't have to look down to know that they were notches – six of them.

CHAPTER 3

BOUNTY HUNTER

The letter made no sense to him at all. Crudely written, it stirred no memories whatsoever.

> Al
> I need 500 bux befor end of month or Im ded. Yeh, yeh, I ws gamblen agen. Sorrie but still need the cash. Yu member that crick when we wus kids an yu fel in – who pulled yu out – Help me Al. Send it thru Reno.
>
> Kip

Definitely brother writing to brother. He had no recollection of a brother, not even a mother or father. And sure not any memory of falling into a creek and being rescued by someone named Kip.

Benbow was sweating, sitting on the edge of the bed. He crumpled the letter, then straightened out the paper and folded it again, pushing it into the grubby envelope. This could be his only link with his past. After staring at it for a while he tossed it on to the bedside table and strode restlessly round the room. He caught a glimpse of himself in a cracked mirror on the wall, paused, and squinted. It was a hard, battered face. Not too bad-looking but its owner had definitely been around. He scratched at the beard, tugged the dark brown hair. Somehow it didn't feel right, like he was used to being more or less clean-shaven.

Doc Gabriel had given him a razor and shaving soap in case he wanted it. He decided now he wanted it.

'Let's see what you really look like,' he said to the reflection and then picked up a bowl and went in search of some hot water.

He had finished shaving and was reading a local newspaper which Gabriel had brought in.

'I need to get out of here, Doc,' he had said at the time, but Gabriel had shaken his head.

'Not just yet, Al. If I let you go I'd be in trouble with Sheriff Heffernan for one thing. For another – well, I don't want to raise your hopes, but there is a man I know who just might be able to help you.'

Benbow had frowned. 'Another doctor?'

Gabriel hesitated then said, 'Not now – he was. But his ways were a little too – radical – and he lost his licence.'

'And you think he can help *me*?'

The doctor seemed uncertain whether to speak or not then merely handed him the paper and started for the door, slowed and turned.

'Bear with me for a couple of days – I really think

you have a chance of regaining your memory.'

Benbow shrugged. 'Guess I got nothing to lose, Doc.'

He found nothing of interest in the local news except that the newly formed Wind River & Prairie Railroad hoped to begin laying track from Cheyenne and Laramie to Lander within three months. There seemed to be some delay about a tunnel through a portion of the Wind River Range that ran across part of the Indian Reserve. And there was quite a public backlash – apparently this was just one of several delays and folk were obviously afraid the railroad extension would never get started. But he wasn't really interested, for none of it meant a thing to him. So he skipped through the story and then looked up as the door opened and Sheriff Howie Heffernan came in, grim-faced as usual.

The sheriff stopped with his hand on the door-knob, frowning at Benbow. Then he came forward, eyes holding to the other man's face. 'You look different without that beard.'

Benbow automatically rubbed a hand over his clean-shaven jowls. 'Feels better – don't think I was used to a beard, somehow.'

'Your face has some tan so I'd say you hadn't had it all that long – and it weren't in the description I got of Al Benbow but the rest of it fits well enough – your size, age, face in general.' The lawman sat down and lifted some papers he held. 'Been in touch with the Laramie law. Seems they know you pretty well up there.' His mouth hardened some and then he said, trying to sound casual, 'Mind if I look at that six-gun?'

Benbow glanced towards the Colt in its holster on the bullet belt that hung over the bed-post. Watching the lawman warily, he reached for it, saw Heffernan casually drop a hand to the butt of his own revolver. Benbow drew the gun out carefully, handed it over butt first.

'Guess you want to check those notches.'

'Uh-huh.' Heffernan took the gun and looked closely at the six notches cut into one edge of the walnut butt which was worn and polished by much handling.

He had wondered what they meant. Was he a gunfighter who kept tab of the men he downed? He couldn't think of anything else, especially remembering the way he had handled those two assassins.

'Six notches – six men dead?'

'No use asking me, Sheriff.'

Heffernan held his gaze steadily. 'Kinda convenient, not bein' able to remember, huh? Specially things like that.'

Benbow said nothing. Heffernan sighed, glanced at his papers again.

'Well, that's what they mean – each notch represents a dead man.'

'What does that make me?' asked Benbow warily. 'A gunfighter?'

Heffernan waited then shook his head slowly. 'Bounty hunter. Seems you like to bring 'em in dead because the 'Dead or Alive' boys are the ones with the biggest bounties.'

Benbow stiffened. 'A bounty hunter?' His voice was no more than a whisper. 'And I live in Laramie?'

'Dunno about that. You *have* been livin' there for a few months, went up into the hills and brought back the body of a man called Braden. Mindless killer, wanted for a long time across three states or territories. Killed several lawmen and a coupla bounty hunters. But seems Al Benbow out-smarted and out-gunned him.' The sheriff flicked his gaze up to Benbow's tight face. 'You must be pretty damn good to track down and shoot it out with someone like that Braden.'

Benbow shook his head slowly. 'Don't recollect, Sheriff . . . mind's still a blank.'

'Like I said – convenient.'

Benbow frowned. 'Why? Something wrong? Bounty hunters ain't usually in trouble when they bring in the bodies, are they?'

'Guess not – depends how far outside the law they stepped. And there ain't a one that I've knowed who did it by the book. They got their eyes on the money more than on the law. But if the one they bring in was really badly wanted' – he shrugged – 'the law can turn a blind eye sometimes.'

'Well, I had nothing but a couple of dollars in my pockets they tell me when Tess Dalton brought me in.'

'It's been three months since you nailed Braden – I'd say you spent it and were lookin' for another target – if it's round here, I want to know about it.'

'How the hell can I tell you a thing like that when I can't even remember my own name?'

'You know what it is – Al Benbow. And no one likes you much. You've bent the law considerable accordin' to the man in Laramie and that brother of yours, Kip, killed a gambler up in Deadwood. Dunno if he notches *his* gun but if he does, that'd make three.'

Benbow continued to stare silently but it was obvious he was shaken by the sheriff's news.

'Killin' seems to run in the family – you want, you can carve two more notches in your gun butt after that little fracas the other night.' Heffernan gestured to the boarded-up window which Gabriel hadn't yet had repaired properly.

There was bitterness in Benbow's tone as he asked, 'There a bounty on 'em?'

'Knew you'd ask that!'

'Knew you were waiting for me to ask it.'

Heffernan coloured, tossed the six-gun on to the bed. 'Don't get sassy with me, or you'll find yourself behind bars, Benbow.'

'You gonna charge me with something?'

The sheriff's eyes slitted and he stood up abruptly. 'I got me a feelin' if I nibble at this long enough, I'll find plenty to charge you with. Meantime, you stay put. Right here.'

He studied Benbow's face for a long moment and then wheeled and left the room, striding impatiently to the door.

Benbow picked up the gun and ran his fingers along the notches on the butt.

Six men – he must have quite a reputation.

Hilton Granger saw Heffernan riding in and turned away from the window quickly and snapped at Jethro Caine.

'Get outa here! He sees that bandage and we're cooked! You know what Heffernan's like. C'mon, damn you! Hurry it up!'

Jethro rolled down his sleeve and grimaced as the cloth rolled tightly across the bandage on his tricep. One of Benbow's bullets had nicked him as he ran away from Gabriel's house and he had kept out of sight and away from the ranch for the last couple of days. He had felt it was safe enough now to show up and tell Granger what had happened – but if he had figured on sympathy from the rancher he was mighty disappointed.

'Christ almighty! A simple job like shootin' a man lyin' in bed and you can't even do that properly!'

That was Granger's greeting as Caine sidled into the room, looking tense and sheepish at the same time.

'Aw, boss, it weren't my fault! Chance didn't shoot fast enough and Smoky weren't worth a damn.'

'You hired 'em! I told you to finish him but, aw, no, you had to go hire a couple of dumb bastards who couldn't hit the side of a barn if they was leanin' against it.'

'I figured if anythin' went wrong and they were caught then we wouldn't be in trouble . . . like they wouldn't trace it back to Circle G.'

Granger all but threw up his arms. 'Chance was *workin'* for Circle G, you blamed idiot!'

Caine shuffled his boots awkwardly. 'Yeah, but he was only roustaboutin', gettin' pocket money for booze. . . . Not like he was on the payroll permanent.'

Grange sat down heavily. 'I just can't think like you, Jethro. You're a good cowman but when it comes to thinkin' things out, you're like a half-wit kid.' Granger frowned suddenly as Caine rolled up his sleeve, revealing part of a bandage. 'What's that. . . ? Goddamnit, don't tell me he wounded you!'

'Just a nick – ricochet from the window frame after he nailed the 'breed – but I think I oughta see a sawbones, boss. It's gettin' red and hurts like hell.'

Granger was on his feet instantly. 'You stay away from the sawbones! Judas, I had Heffernan out here askin' about Chance and I managed to convince him Chance'd left the afternoon of the shootin', but—'

'Hey! I think that's Heff ridin' in now!' exclaimed Jethro, crouching to see through the window.

That was when Granger roared at him to get the hell out and stay out of sight. As he pushed the man out of the office door he snarled, 'You better hope no one saw you in town that night!'

But Hilton Granger seemed calm enough and busy with a cattle ledger when Sheriff Heffernan walked in, thumbing back his hat. It looked normal enough in the ranch office.

'Thought that was you ridin' through the gate, Howie,' the rancher said amiably enough. He set down his pen and rubbed his eyes as if he had been working on the books for hours. 'Damn paperwork . . . rather be brush-poppin' mavericks again. Figure I work harder now than when I first started this spread.'

'Reckon you'd be makin' more though,' Heffernan opined, dropping unasked into a chair. He started to build a cigarette with his long bony fingers. 'This feller Benbow . . .'

Granger looked exasperated. 'Look, Howie, I already told you, I don't know him, and Chance was only roustaboutin' here for booze money – I've no idea why he might've wanted to take a shot at Benbow in one of

Doc Gabriel's beds. I've got too much work to do for just jawin' about it, so if I can help, *really* help you in any way, just get it said and we'll take it from there.'

Heffernan took his time rolling the cigarette, ran his tongue along the edge of the paper, looking upwards at the rancher. He twisted it into shape, smoothing the cylinder several times, seeing Granger's mouth tighten.

He scraped a vesta alight on a boot sole and exhaled a long plume of smoke, flicking the dead match at the ashtray on the desk. Granger scowled when it missed, picked it up and dropped it in.

'I'm waitin', Howie, but time's a'wastin'.'

'Gil Dancey at the livery says Jethro's hoss was in town that night.'

The rancher frowned. 'Which night was that?'

Heffernan didn't answer, merely stared until Granger nodded irritably. 'All right, all right, you're talkin' about the night this Benbow got shot at, I guess – I dunno why the hell you're botherin' me with this but if Jethro was in town, you'd best ask him about it. Like I told you the other day, he's been up in the hills on round-up and if he wants to slip into town for a beer or a woman that's OK by me, long as he's back on the job the next day. He don't ask my permission so, like I said, you'd better ask him about it.'

'Yeah, well, I'll do that when I see him – just that he buys Chance and that 'breed a drink now and again.'

'Hell, most of my men do – they're a sorry pair. Or were.'

'Yeah. That Benbow: he's deadly with a Colt. Got six notches on the butt.'

Granger stiffened. 'Hell! He's a gunfighter?'

Heffernan shook his head, told the rancher what he had learned about a man named Al Benbow from Laramie. Granger listened closely, eased back in his chair, tapping his fingers on the arm of the chair.

'Bounty hunter – you sure?'

'Accordin' to Marshal Hunsecker in Laramie and he's a damn good lawman. I'd take his word.'

'Well, well, well.' Granger suddenly seemed more relaxed and he heaved out of the chair and went to a cupboard, brought out a bottle of whiskey and two glasses.

The sheriff looked mildly surprised as he was handed a drink.

'You look like you can use a drink for the road, Howie – toss it down. You'll find Jethro somewhere round the bunkhouse I reckon. Took a fall from his hoss and hurt his shoulder so I told him to take it easy.'

Heffernan drained his glass and wiped a hand across his thin lips. 'You seem to favour Jethro some.'

Granger laughed easily. 'Ask him that and he'll deny it. No. It's just that good cowmen like Jethro are hard to come by. Plenty of grubline riders and ordinary cowpokes, but a man who knows cattle like Jethro Caine – well, it's worth bendin' the rules a little to keep him happy.'

Heffernan nodded and headed for the door. He opened it but looked back at Granger. 'Just don't sound like you, Hilt, that's all.'

Granger's smile stiffened a little but it didn't disappear. 'There are lots of sides to me you ain't seen yet, Howie.'

'Yeah – I reckon. Thanks for the drink.'

'So Benbow's a bounty hunter – and I hear Chance was bitchin' that some friend of his was killed by a lousy bounty hunter not long ago. Maybe it was Benbow and now you know why Chance tried to blast him with a shotgun. . . .'

'Good theory, Hilt, worth thinkin' about.'

Heffernan went out and Granger watched him all the way across the yard to the bunkhouse. He paced the floor impatiently waiting for the sheriff to appear again and ride out. When he did, he waited even more impatiently for Jethro to come up to the house.

'The hell was he talkin' to you about for so long?' Granger demanded.

'Aw, this and that – mostly about Chance and why he'd want to kill Benbow. I said if he was a bounty hunter, he was bound to've made a lot of enemies, kin of men he'd killed and so on. Said I thought Chance mentioned once he had somethin' to square with a bounty hunter, but he didn't mention his name. . . .'

Granger arched his eyebrows. 'My God! And I told him almost the same thing. How did you come up with a thing like that and still be dumb enough to make a mess of killin' Benbow?'

Caine shrugged, looking a trifle hurt. 'I dunno – just come into my head. . . . What we do about Benbow now, boss?'

'Nothin'.'

Caine's eyes widened. '*Nothin'*!'

'No. He ain't who we thought he was – he's only a damn bounty hunter. He ain't no worry to us. Sure, keep an eye on him, but my bet is he'll be outa here mighty soon – and with no memory! That's the bonus, Jethro, he don't recollect a damn thing. And a lousy bounty hunter won't keep me awake nights. Nah, we can forget about Benbow bein' a danger to us. Come and have a drink on the strength of it.'

After they'd downed the good whiskey and Caine was smacking his lips, the rancher said, 'You see this week's paper?' Caine shook his head: he wasn't a reading man. 'Piece in about the railroad and that mountain – they got it wrong but it's more or less along the lines we told that reporter. Lot of folk are riled at the delay. . . .'

Jethro looked at his boss steadily. 'Must still be waitin' for that geologist's report, I guess.'

Granger gave a crooked smile, glanced at a locked drawer of his desk.

'Yeah, wouldn't wonder. But with people gettin' hot under the collar, now's a good time to bring a little more pressure on Lacy.'

Their eyes met and Jethro held out his glass for a refill. Granger hesitated, but slopped some whiskey into the glass.

'You mean. . . ?'

'You know what I mean.'

Jethro Caine smiled and lifted the glass in a kind of salute.

' 'Course I do. Luck, boss.'

'And lots of it,' Granger said a mite stiffly, a cloud of worry just hazing his eyes as he drank.

CHAPTER 4

NIGHT RIDERS

The raiders came with the setting of the moon.

Greg Lacy's prime herd was being fattened on his best pasture on the banks of the Wind River and he had set three nighthawks to watch over the cattle. They were good men, knew their jobs and were as loyal as most forty-and-found cowpokes. Which meant they would ride for the brand and even trade a little lead with the ranch's enemies but not necessarily lay down their lives.

Still, top-hand Cass Doubleday was a strong-minded *hombre* and had been riding herd on ranchers' cows for nigh on thirty years. He knew a good boss when he saw one and Greg Lacy was about as good as a man could get out here in the mostly lawless land of Wyoming. Winters were bitter and summers were hot and fly-ridden, but Lacy worked his men fairly, expected – as was his right – that they would go the extra mile on his behalf in return for good grub, warm beds and regular pay.

Doubleday had pared down the crew until he had a group of hard-working cowpokes, contented with their lot. He knew he could call on them to stand by Lacy and his pretty young wife if necessary – and a lot of the loyalty they had, Cass knew, was because of Libby Lacy. She was a fine-looking young woman, always had a smile for the men, traded jokes with them, and served up some of the best grub they had ever tasted. She helped those who couldn't write with letters to far-off families, was teaching two of the men to read and write more than just their names.

He would bet that the crew he bossed for Greg would risk their lives for the young rancher.

But when the masked raiders came thundering out of the night, riding through the small camp, shooting and yelling, he wasn't so sure.

Doubleday and Carey Watt were catching a cup of java while Sting Laker rode herd, crooning some off-key melody to keep the cattle reassured. The two men were holding the tin mugs of coffee between their hands, blowing on the liquid to cool it so they could get back to their stations quickly.

Then the night exploded into chaos around them and Carey Watt jumped up, spilling his coffee unnoticed, stood there rigidly, wide-eyed, as horsemen came out of the dark. First they dropped a loop over the buckboard that held the bedrolls and supplies, hauling it up on to two wheels and past the point of balance until it overturned with a crash. Another man had cut the remuda loose and horses squealed and snorted and plunged in terror as guns blasted near them.

But Carey Watt just stood there as riders surged past him until one man leaned from the saddle and slammed his rifle barrel across Watt's head, knocking him sprawling.

Cass Doubleday had dived for his rifle where it was propped against a log, fumbled badly and dropped the weapon. He rolled on to his back, dragging his six-gun free, shooting at the wild, dark shapes above him. But he fired too soon and the bullet whipped away into the night, heading for the stars.

Gun flame stabbed down at him and he slammed back, feeling the hammer blow in his shoulder as it spilled him awkwardly.

'Carey!' he bawled. 'Use your gun!'

But there was no gunfire coming from Watt's position. The dazed cowpoke sat up, rubbing at his throbbing head, not really aware of what was happening. Then he screamed as a galloping horse crashed into him and trampled him underfoot, his body jerking and twisting on the ground as a second set of hoofs tore at his flesh and bones.

Doubleday saw it and swore as he fought to one knee. But a horse drove into him with such force that he was sent spinning a couple of yards and consciousness fled as he crashed on to his face, his mouth full of dirt and grass.

The raiders rode on clear through the camp – and by that time, Sting Laker was spurring back towards the campsite, rifle in hand, yelling.

'Cass! Carey! What the hell's happenin'?' He reined down, seeing the overturned wagon, lifted his rifle.

There was a ragged volley of gunfire. Luckily for Laker the weapons weren't all aimed at him – some were shooting into the air, setting the already nervous cattle milling and bawling until one took the lead. They stampeded.

They ran for the river and Laker brought up his rifle, shooting wildly, just as fast as he could work lever and trigger. A horse slammed into his mount and Laker yelled as he jarred from the saddle, snatching at the horn in a desperate attempt to keep from falling into the heaving steers now surrounding him. A rifle barrel knocked his hat flying and dragged across his scalp, splitting the skin and sending a wave of warm blood down into his eyes. He was almost blinded but his biggest worry was that he was going down now – into the stampeding herd.

He fell on to the heaving, hairy backs, miraculously missing the jerking horns. His body was flung from one steer to another, his hoarse cries lost in the thundering, snorting horror of the mindless, rushing cattle.

Finally, he disappeared – but the herd surged on without pause, the front of the wedge already smashing through the strand-wire fence, into the muddy river, churning it, writhing and heaving as deep mud sucked at forelegs and gripped like a closing fist.

Those still charging out of the pasture, eyes white-edged and rolling, nostrils wet and snorting, throats roaring like demons from Hell, thrust the balking herd-front forward, over the bank, on top of those already trapped.

The pile-up seemed endless, the primitive mindless fear that had gripped the cattle refusing to allow them to halt their mad charge. . . .

Sitting sweating horses back up the slope a little, one of the raiders wiped an arm across his damp face and said, 'That's about it, boys. Let's head for town to celebrate!'

Hurd Satterlee and Chick Rendell had put away a bottle and a half of raw rotgut, belly-churning whiskey between them.

They had used up all their money and what little credit the saloon was prepared to advance them and the painted women turned their backs when they tried to sweet-talk them into taking them upstairs.

'We'll pay come payday,' Satterlee assured a henna-haired, busty whore, clinging to her flabby arm.

She turned, placed a well-padded foot on the end of a soft but heavy leg against his chest and kicked him away. Hurd fell sprawling out of his chair, taking it down with him, and Chick found it amusing, laughing so that he had trouble keeping his feet.

Satterlee scowled. 'Shut up!' he snarled at his pard. 'It ain't funny!'

'Is from where I'm standin'.'

'Well, keep laughin' an' you won't be standin' for long!'

Chick couldn't stop laughing and the henna-haired beauty grabbed him by the neck and, to a roar from the mostly drunken crowd in the bar-room, threw Chick on top of Hurd.

Satterlee took that as an attack and clumsily threw

a punch which landed on Chick's nose. Rendell howled and floundered across to beat at his one-time pard. But by that time the saloon's bouncers were on the job and they both ended up in the back alley, skidding through the garbage and muck amongst the empty crates and piles of bottles.

They slid in a huddled heap against the clapboard wall of the privy and, as the bouncers moved back, three big dark shapes stepped out. One man was tugging his chamois work gloves tighter on his hands and then he reached into a pocket and handed the nearest bouncer some coins. The man nodded, and he and his sidekick went back into the saloon. The trio stopped just beside the cowboys who were clawing at each other drunkenly.

'Nice of you boys to get yourselves into position for us,' said the one who had paid off the bouncers.

'Huh?' slurred Satterlee, squinting up at the men standing over him and Chick Rendell. 'Wha—?'

'Nah, don't move. Just – stay – *put*!'

On the last word the man drove a boot into Hurd's chest, knocking him back against the wall. The drunken cowboy moaned sickly.

'Hey!' yelled Chick, trying vainly to get his rubbery legs under him. 'You can't do that to my pard!'

'I can – and I can do it to you, too – see?'

The big boot drove savagely against the side of Chick Rendell's head and he went down with a sick, slobbering sound, moaning like a graveyard ghost.

'Judas! We ain't s'posed to kill 'em, are we, Jeth—?'

The man who spoke had the words crammed back

into his teeth as Jethro Caine's gloved fist swung up in a backhand blow. 'Get doin' what you're bein' paid to do! Or you'll find yourself on the ground with these two!'

The two men moved in, boots kicking and driving soddenly into the two men huddled against the wall. Grunts and moans were smothered by the smack of the blows. Jethro twisted his fingers in the hair of Satterlee, hauled the man half-erect, Hurd crying out as he felt hair tearing out of his scalp.

'Clear out of Wind River, Satterlee! Get right away from here and take Rendell with you. We see you still ridin' for Lacy come daylight and we'll shoot you outa the saddle!'

He drove a knee into the man's face, the back of Satterlee's skull crunching against the wall. He continued to hold the hair and hammered four sickening blows into the man's destroyed face.

The other two had stood back and now Caine, panting, rounded on them, flinging an arm towards the battered men.

'Kick 'em! Kick 'em till I tell you to stop!' he gritted. '*Do it!* Or I'll shoot you both!'

The men knew better than to argue with Jethro Caine when he was in one of his bloody moods.

They closed on the huddled heap of the two cowboys, hesitated briefly, then began kicking rhythmically. Jethro leaned his beefy shoulders against the saloon wall, tugged off his blood-soaked gloves with his teeth and stuffed them into his belt.

Then he took cigarette papers and tobacco from his shirt pocket and began making a smoke.

He sniffed and spat. 'What I call a good night's work, eh, boys?'

Howie Heffernan looked irritated and unsettled as he snapped his head up and glared across his cluttered desk.

Hilton Granger came storming into his office, wearing range clothes that looked as if he had slept in them – which he had – and been torn by bushes and hard riding: which they had, also. He was followed by Jethro Caine who looked as if he had been up all night and two more Circle G hands stood on the stoop, waiting.

'Come on, Howie – I need you out on my range. I been hit by goddamn rustlers!'

Heffernan stiffened with a jerk. 'Hell, not you, too!'

'What d'you mean, *too*?' demanded Granger, frowning.

'The Lacy place was hit last night. Not so much rustlers as a raid. Stampeded his herd, intentionally or otherwise, and it piled-up in the river. Lost twenty-three head, all prime stuff.'

'Judas priest! We—'

'Then two of his men were beat-up in town behind the Trailman saloon. Fact, looks like Hurd Satterlee's goin' to die, but Chick Rendell might make it, Doc Gabriel says.'

Granger stared and then threw out his arms. 'The hell's happenin' in your bailiwick, Howie! This ain't the usual thing.'

'Damn right it ain't and it ain't gonna happen

again if I can help it. You lose some cows, I take it?'

' 'Bout a dozen – Jethro and some of the boys trailed 'em up into the hills but lost 'em.' Granger looked concerned. 'But, hell, it don't seem much after what happened to Lacy – Greg'd be pretty upset, wouldn't he?'

'He's pretty damn mad. He was short of men as it was. Not because no one wants to work for him, but because he ain't got the money to hire, way I heard it.'

'Well, I knew he was operatin' on a shoestring. I sent a couple boys over last round-up he did to lend a hand. Still, if the railroad gets the OK to tunnel through that mountain on Greg's land it ought to set him up. . . . You gonna go after them rustlers, Howie, or you just gonna sit here bitchin' about what a tough job you've got?'

Heffernan nodded, eyes slitted, tight-lipped. 'Gonna take out a posse – Carey Watts and Sting Laker were killed in the stampede.'

'Christ almighty!' Granger scowled at Jethro, rounding on the ramrod. 'Too damn bad you lost the trail!'

Caine shrugged, looking worried. 'There's Injuns still in them hills, boss. Might've even been some of them that hit us. Whoever it was, sure knew how to cover tracks – I don't think you'll find anythin', Howie.'

Heffernan was checking a rifle he had taken down from some wall pegs. 'I gotta look. You comin' with us, Hilt?'

Granger hadn't been expecting that but after the

act he had put on he really couldn't refuse. 'Damn right!' he said, hoping he sounded enthusiastic. 'Jethro and a couple boys can come, too, but I need to leave the others at the spread.'

'OK – well, let's get goin'. We'll pick up Greg at the undertaker's.'

'Think Chick'll make it?' Jethro asked, casually, and the sheriff looked at him hard as he jammed his hat on his head.

'He better. . . .' The sheriff gestured towards Caine's whipcord trousers. 'That dried blood? You got it on your boots and gloves, too.'

Caine looked down and nodded readily enough. 'We been castratin' maverick bulls.'

Heffernan took his time in sliding his gaze away from the big man with the brutal, unshaven face, then nodded curtly and shouldered past him and the two cowboys standing on the stoop.

'Let's get on the trail.'

Jethro Caine winked at the sober Granger and hitched at his gun-belt before following the lawman outside.

Granger moved more slowly: sometimes Jethro was just a mite too cocky. He was afraid that one of these days it would be the undoing of them all.

CHAPTER 5

HIRED HAND

Benbow sat on the edge of his bed smoking, looking at the back of the young woman sitting beside one of the other three beds in the small infirmary. She was Libby Lacy, a local rancher's wife, according to Doc Gabriel when he had introduced Benbow to her.

She was a handsome woman but kind of distracted. She had come to see the two battered cowhands who had been brought in during the night. One had died, someone named Satterlee, and a blood-spotted sheet covered his body on the corner bed. The other cowhand was swathed in bandages, his breathing heavy and wet-sounding. The woman was holding one of his limp hands.

She was talking quietly to him and looked around, startled, when the door opened and a harassed looking man in his mid-twenties came in quickly, carrying a rifle. The woman half-rose out of her chair.

'Doc told me about Hurd.' Greg Lacy's dark eyes

went to the body on the other bed. He was narrow-faced, boyish, but he looked determined now with his lips drawn in a thin, tight line. 'Heffernan's getting up a posse and I'm riding with 'em.'

Libby looked a little startled but covered quickly and said, quietly, 'D'you think it was Indians?'

'Might be – out on the range, anyway.' He looked pointedly at the injured man. 'How's Chick doing?'

She shook her head very slightly but said aloud, 'He's making good progress, Doc said.'

Lacy grunted. 'I been all round town – no one wants to work for me now. Two men dead in the stampede, another here from a kicking, and Chick a walking example of what can happen if you work for Lazy L. No wonder Cass Doubleday quit.'

Libby drew in a sharp breath. 'Greg! What d'you mean "if you work for Lazy L"?'

'Don't seem to me like Chick and Hurd got into any drunken brawl. I been around enough to know an expert beating when I see one. The whole thing was set up – agin Lazy L.'

The girl was white now, a hand at her throat. 'But – who'd want to drive our men off? And why?'

'I aim to find out when I get back. With luck we'll have the men who did it all: stampeded the herd, killed my cowhands, and beat-up on Chick.'

She sighed heavily and Benbow admired her. He could see she didn't like any of this, but she wasn't about to try to stop her husband going on the posse: she knew it had to be done and he had to go.

'Meantime, we're terribly short-handed,' she said. 'We'll never round-up more cattle to replace those we lost before market time, Greg.'

He nodded as he stepped forward and kissed her black hair. 'I know, Libby. One good tophand would help a lot but men are scared off now. You can't blame 'em.'

'I'll work for you.'

They snapped their heads around as Benbow stood up, walked across and thrust out his right hand. 'Al Benbow – so they tell me.'

Greg Lacy gripped and said his name, studying Benbow closely. 'You're the gunfighter with no memory.'

'Bounty hunter, according to Heffernan – no, can't remember anything much. But I – *know* I can handle cattle.'

Lacy looked dubious. 'Might be – might be I can use you – but I have to tell you, you'll have to wait for your pay till after I sell my herd. Or what's left of it.'

Benbow shrugged. 'That's OK – I just feel I've got to do something. Doc's got some plan he's hatching, but I can't sit around here waiting. We got a deal or not?'

Lacy frowned some: he didn't like being pushed. 'For now – as long as Doc OKs it.'

'He don't have all the say,' Benbow told him.

Lacy glanced at Libby and although she hesitated, she nodded, still watching Benbow. 'I hear your gun is – notched, Mr Benbow.'

'Call me Al – yeah. Six men, according to Heffernan. I don't recall.'

'You be willing to use that gun on behalf of my ranch – the Lazy L?' Lacy asked quietly.

Benbow's gaze was steady. 'I'll stand up for you long as you're paying my wages.'

'You sound mighty certain of that.'

Benbow shrugged. 'Something else I just know.'

Greg Lacy hesitated a little longer then thrust out his right hand. 'OK – if Doc says so. You can ride out with Libby.'

Doc Gabriel wasn't too pleased.

'You have to realize your skull is still pressing on your brain,' he told Benbow seriously. 'You can't go doing too much physical labour. It could start internal bleeding again and that could well prove fatal.'

'Doc, the way I am now, I'm nothing – I've got no past and not much future – the kind I'd want to look forward to, leastways. I'm willing to take the chance.'

'That may be but my friend I spoke to you about should arrive within the next few days – I'd be a lot happier if you'd wait.'

Benbow asked shrewdly, 'He going to relieve this pressure you're worried about?'

'Well, no, but I do hope he'll give you at least some of your memory back.'

'How come only some?'

Gabriel's teeth tugged briefly at his lower lip. 'Well, I'm fairly confident he'll be able to stir recent memories, but – as I mentioned his ideas are a little radical and haven't been developed fully. It's just a chance I think is worth your taking.'

'A risk?'

'Not much but – yes, some risk.'

Benbow lifted his arms out from his sides. 'Like if I went to work for Lazy L?'

'Rather – less. But—'

'You can send for me when your friend gets here, Doc – OK?'

Gabriel knew when he had met a really stubborn man and gave in. Greg Lacy said he had to go and hurried out. Libby looked down at Chick who was sleeping now.

'Doc, you'll let me know right away if there's any change? For better or – worse?'

'I'll do that, Libby – and try to keep this damn fool on some sort of rein, will you?'

She gave Benbow a half-smile. 'I think that might be kind of difficult. . . .'

When Lacy told the waiting posse the news, Hilton Granger and Jethro Caine exchanged looks and the rancher said, 'How come this bounty hunter reckons he knows cattle but can't remember his own name?'

'Don't ask me. Doc says it's just some instinct that tells him. I'm desperate for men now so I'm willing to take a chance.'

'You be able to pay him?'

Greg Lacy narrowed his eyes at Granger. 'My finances are my business, Hilt.'

Granger shrugged, smiling faintly. 'Sure – just thinkin' that if you're strapped down after losin' them cattle and the men, maybe I could help out. Just bein' neighbourly.'

Lacy flushed. 'I know, Hilt – sorry. I'm pretty damn edgy. It'll be rough, but I figure we might be able to manage – if Benbow's the tophand he claims to be.'

'Top gun, more like it,' murmured Jethro, catching the hard look the sheriff threw him. 'Well, a man who notches his gun butt. . . . What d'you reckon?'

Heffernan scowled. 'Forget that *nothing man* right now. Let's see if we can pick up the trail of those killers.'

The posse was ten-strong, grim-faced, and included a couple of cowboys sent over by other valley ranchers to help out.

With Heffernan riding out front, wanting to be alone as he planned his strategy, they moved their mounts to a lope along the trail, lifting into the first of the foothills.

The Lazy L was a good-looking ranch, Benbow decided, as he stopped his big buckskin on the rise and leaned his arms on the saddle horn. Libby Lacy, riding a little ahead, swung her mount back alongside, looking concerned.

'Are you all right, Al?'

He grinned. 'I'm fine. Headache's no worse'n hangovers I've had.' He gestured to the neat buildings and corrals of the ranch below and still half a mile off. The surrounding country was green and lush-looking, giving way to a purple-hazed range with the river glinting off to the west. 'Good spot – far enough back from the river if it floods, plenty of good grass, high country easily accessible for the herds. Small bunkhouse, though. How many hands you got?'

Her full red lips compressed slightly. 'We did have six men – three died last night . . . and I don't think Chick will ever work for us again when he recovers.'

There was a catch in her voice now although she tried hard to cover it. 'I just can't believe it! It's all happened so fast.'

'You've never had this kind of trouble before?'

'Never. This is a good valley, peaceful, rich, with good people in it—'

'The railroad's coming, isn't it? I read it in some paper Doc gave me.' He smiled ruefully. 'I can recollect that far back.'

Her face softened. 'It must be awful, not being able to recall your past.'

'I've felt . . . easier,' he admitted. 'Night time's the worst. When there's no distractions. You keep thinking and worrying and – wondering.'

'The notches on your gun must have given you something of a jolt.'

'Yeah. First thing I thought of was "gunfighter". But Heffernan found out that Al Benbow is a bounty hunter. Given a choice, I'm not sure just which one I'd prefer to be.'

Bounty hunters were not always regarded as the best kind of citizens. A gunfighter might inspire a sense of awe, but a man who kills for cold hard cash – blood money. . . .

'To answer your question, Al, yes, the railroad is thinking of coming out here – well, I guess it is coming for sure, but they're trying to make up their minds just where the track will go.'

'They gonna run right through the valley?'

'Yes – that's the plan. Providing they can drive a tunnel through that mountain there – the one with the broken pines on top?'

She gestured to the closest part of the range and he saw it was this side of the river.

'That's on your range?'

'Yes. If they can drive a tunnel through safely they'll come out on to Circle G land and have a more or less direct link to Lander, cutting straight through.'

'Was something in the paper about having to cross the Indian Reservation.'

She frowned. 'I read that – but it's not right. Some reporter got it wrong, I guess. We're south of the reservation here and with the tunnel, the line would run across Circle G and two other ranches to the north, missing the reservation altogether.'

'What if they decided not to tunnel through?'

'Well. . . .' She smiled wryly. 'To be honest, we'd miss out on a hefty compensation pay-out and I'm afraid we've been counting on that rather heavily. But the line would have to skirt the range, which, of course, would be far more costly, and while it would still take in some of Circle G, the other ranchers would miss out because it would have to swing south of them, due to the nature of the country.'

Benbow grunted, rubbed his head. He understood what she was saying but his head sure was pounding.

'When they gonna make a decision about the tunnel?'

Libby looked uncomfortable. 'I can't say. There was a geologist here, a pleasant man but obviously a worrier. Mr Church, Ashley Church. . . . He did some drilling and minor blasting, testing the strength of the rock – strata? Is that the word?'

'I'll take your word for it.' She saw how tight his mouth was and knew his mind must be in turmoil as he tried hard to comprehend what she was telling him.

'I'm sorry – I don't mean to confuse you. Mr Church was making tests, the results of which were secret, of course. He was staying on the ranch here and rode into town to send off his report – and we haven't seen him since.' She lowered her voice as she added, 'Neither has anyone else.'

'What? He disappeared?'

Her smile was forced. 'Oh, I don't think that's quite the right word. But the local postal agent swears he never saw Church that day and he didn't board the stage. Greg believes he decided to hand-deliver his report instead of trusting the mails and rode out to Laramie.' She frowned again. 'He had a rather distinctive mount, an Appaloosa, very dark in the rear so that the spots stood out – but no one recalls seeing anyone riding such a horse, either.'

'Sounds to me like he didn't make it to Laramie.'

'Don't say that! We – we need the railroad to drill that tunnel or – or – I don't know what we'll do! We took a chance – Mr Church told us his preliminary tests proved good – and we borrowed money. The bank loaned it on the strength of that tunnel going through.'

Benbow grimaced, face contorting. 'Ma'am – I – I guess I better not keep talking about this. My head feels like it's about to explode. . . .'

'Oh! I'm sorry! I run on, but it's only because I'm so worried. Let's hurry on down and I'll make you some strong coffee. Greg keeps a bottle of whiskey. You might like some added to your coffee?'

He forced a smile. 'Ma'am, I'll be your slave for life!'

Howie Heffernan stood up from beside the sodden trail and looked at Granger and Jethro through the rain.

'Well, I ain't seen tracks covered as well as this.' He gestured down the slope of the mountain. 'And it ain't all because of the rain. Some sign of tramplin' down there, but I can't find another damn thing.' Heffernan wasn't only the sheriff of the county, he was also the best tracker for hundreds of miles around, having once been an Indian Scout for the army. 'How many head you reckon you lost, Hilt?'

'Ten or a dozen – look, if you can't find tracks, Howie, there can't be none there,' Granger said. He let his gaze stray up the rain-hazed slope. 'Looks to me like it might've been a bunch of renegade bucks from the reservation. Wouldn't be the first time they got drunk on that rotgut they brew and hit us settlers. And if it was them, you'll have hell's own job gettin' to 'em the way that Indian Agency is.'

'Injuns don't waste beef. If they're takin' the trouble to rustle it, they don't stampede it into the river and let the cows pile up and kill themselves.'

'Might've done that to keep the cowpokes busy,' Jethro said.

Heffernan threw him a cold look. 'You work that out all by yourself, Jethro? Man, they *killed* all but one of the nighthawks. Who they tryin' to decoy?'

Jethro flushed but shrugged.

'Well, Howie, I didn't lose enough steers to make it worth my while spendin' a lot of time here,' Granger said. 'I'll take Jethro, leave you my other three men, and you can stay on – we got plenty to do back at the ranch.' He gestured to the men he had brought to the posse. 'I'll want these boys back at work by tomorrow, whether you find anythin' or not.'

Heffernan nodded slowly. 'Seems you were the hardest hit, Greg.'

Lacy had been watching Granger closely, too, and now shifted his gaze to the lawman. 'Yeah – I'm inclined to go along with you, Howie. This don't have the Injun touch. I lost more'n twenty head of prime beef I couldn't afford to lose and, God help me, three good men. Seems like more'n a coincidence to me my herds being hit and my men beat-up all in the one night.'

'Hell, Chick and Satterlee were in some kinda drunken brawl, weren't they?' Granger said harshly.

'They were drunk,' Lacy admitted. 'I gave them a small advance on their pay because they'd been out on the brush for ten days rounding-up. They weren't brawlers, never made much trouble – you can back me on that, Howie.'

'Well, I tossed 'em in the cells a few times but not any more than I did other cowpokes. You sayin' somethin' I ain't quite caught, Greg?'

Lacy seemed uncertain now at the direct question. 'Well – I dunno. It just don't sit right. We had no trouble the first coupla years here. Only after the railroad said they'd drive a line through the valley things started to go wrong.'

They waited for him to continue.

'Hell, I can't put my finger on anything special! But fences would get broken; cows and horses would wander on to loco weed; there'd be small brushfires – one wiped out a linecamp – lots of things like that.'

'Hell, that's part of ranchin' in this country, Greg,' said Granger. 'Them things happen all the time. You're beginnin' to sound like a man who's thinkin' of quittin'.'

Lacy turned his head slowly. 'I never let myself think that before, but when men are getting killed. . . !'

'You're jumpin' to conclusions,' growled Heffernan, 'And we're wastin' time here.'

Granger lifted a finger towards Lacy. 'Greg, tell you what: if you're serious about quittin', you get your spread valued – and I'll double it.'

Lacy jumped. '*Double* it!'

The others stared too, but Granger seemed at ease. 'Yeah. Normally I wouldn't want your spread, but with the railroad pushin' through – well, it could mean a lot to me, them crossin' my land – and if I had the mountain, they'd compensate me for that as well. You could pay off your big bank loan and come out ahead, I reckon, start afresh where you'd feel Libby was safe.'

Greg Lacy stared, brow creased, water dripping from his hatbrim. He was worried about Libby's safety, deep down. He *knew* those men had been deliberately beaten, though he couldn't prove it. And, of course, his nighthawks had been killed in cold blood. It was getting too dangerous for someone like Libby. But they'd worked hard to get this place built up to what it was. The railroad money would be a godsend – providing the tunnel was given the OK. . . .

'Just think about it for a coupla days, Greg,' Granger said reasonably. 'Let me know – I'll keep the offer open for a week. Fair enough?'

CHAPTER 6

RANCH HAND OR GUN HAND?

There was a strange feeling out here on the Lazy L, thought Benbow, as he stood in the bunkhouse doorway, rolling a cigarette.

It was as if it was familiar – vaguely – but somehow he knew he had never seen this ranch before coming out with Libby. He decided it was the fact that he had worked ranches before and it was the *feel* of the place that he was experiencing. He might not be able to recall details, but the overall atmosphere was working on him and he knew he had been a cowhand at some time in the past.

He had told Greg that he had worked many ranches and at the time it had seemed to be the truth, something that just came into his mind and felt – right. But he hadn't been all that sure on the ride out and hoped he wouldn't make a fool of himself – or let Greg Lacy down.

The two cowhands still working the place – Larry McMartin and Hec Munro, the horse wrangler, seemed warily friendly – but definitely a trifle leery of him. Maybe it was the notches on his gunbutt or merely the fact that he was a man in limbo and they didn't know just how to treat him.

He lit his cigarette, watched Hec saddle a horse down by the corral and check that he had his Winchester in the scabbard. Larry had already ridden out. Benbow flicked away the dead match and started up towards the house.

Libby came out on to the porch and waved, smiling warmly. She was a nice-looking young woman, he thought, genuinely friendly. Which was not necessarily a really good thing out here. Some men could mistake that smile for something more than just friendliness.

What the hell was he thinking along those lines for?

Before he could answer himself – if there was an answer – she said, 'How are you with tools, Al? There's a good deal of fencing that needs attention.'

'Reckon I can handle it.'

Her smile faded slightly. 'Are you sure?'

'I'm sure. Look, Libby, I just have this feeling that I know ranch work. If I foul-up, I'll ride out without any fuss.'

'Oh, I don't think there'll be any need for anything as drastic as that.'

'I like to give a good day's work for a day's pay,' he said, and once again he didn't know where the words had come from. It just seemed – right. He grinned.

'Show me the tool shed and I'll see how I do. . . .'

Half an hour later, he was reining down not far from the river, seeing the sagging fencing and the splintered posts and rails and the churned-up ground where the wrecked buckboard lay, some of the supplies still scattered around, beyond saving.

This must be where the rustlers hit. Standing in the stirrups, he saw where the river-bank had broken down and saw the carcasses of the dead animals piled up by some rocks. Larry McMartin was splashing coal oil over the corpses and Benbow reached for his neckerchief, pulled it up over his nose and mouth.

In minutes there was pungent black smoke rising and Larry came riding back. He was a little younger than Benbow, his wolfish face now tight, the high cheekbones very prominent.

'Gonna stink us out while we work on the fence.'

Benbow hadn't realized Larry would be working with him. 'Wind's blowing away from us so it mightn't be too bad— Might've been best to leave it till we were through, though.'

McMartin looked at him soberly. 'Evenin' breeze blows towards the house. And I make my own decisions, mister.'

'Good way to be. We gonna get started on the fence?'

'You get started – I'm gonna have me a smoke first.' He rode back into the shade of some trees and dismounted, back to a tree trunk, taking his time building a cigarette. Testing me! Benbow thought, his expression deadpan as he unloaded his tools, walked over to a splintered post and began digging around it with the pickaxe.

It was a warm day and would get hotter as the sun climbed the sky. Some lines of thickening clouds showed along the range, some with a tinge of grey. In fact, it looked like it might even be raining some up in the hills.

Larry hadn't moved from the shade by the time Benbow had loosened the lower part of the splintered post and pulled it out. He had finished his smoke but just sat there, watching Benbow work.

'We need some new posts.'

Larry spread his hands. 'Then go cut 'em – plenty of saplin's around here.'

Benbow leaned on the pickaxe, blotted sweat from his face with his shirt sleeve. 'You're closer,' he said finally.

The smirk disappeared from Larry's face and he glared for a few moments before heaving to his feet. He sauntered across and stood in front of Benbow, hands on hips.

'You don't order me around, dummy.'

'Who's ordering? Just stating a fact. Besides the axe is propped against the tree where you were smoking.'

Larry leaned forward a little from the waist. 'Well, go get it! Start swingin' . . . I might start unrollin' the wire in a little while. I feel like takin' it easy today.'

He turned abruptly but stopped when Benbow said, 'Now who's ordering?'

Larry turned sharply. 'Listen, you're the new man and I don't care whether you say you can remember or not. But you do what me and Hec say, OK?'

Benbow shook his head. 'I'll do what Libby and Greg tell me to – you two can go climb up your own nose.'

That shook Larry and he was speechless for a moment, then his eyes bulged. His right arm twitched and he paused. *This ranny was leaning on the pickaxe with both hands – he wouldn't be able to reach his gun before Larry could draw. . . .*

Larry was wrong.

He tried, but before his gun's chamber had cleared the top of the holster he was staring down the barrel of Benbow's six-gun – the one with the notched butt, Larry remembered with a sudden sick feeling. He let his gun drop back into leather and held his hands out from his sides.

'Take – take it easy, feller!'

'Figured I was. You're the one tried to drag iron.'

Larry's smile was sickly. Sweat dripped from his angular jawline. 'Just . . . testin' you! No harm meant, I swear!'

'You live dangerously, kid.' The Colt disappeared into Benbow's holster as fast as it had appeared in his right hand.

'You are a gunfighter, ain't you?' There was a touch of awe in Larry's words but Benbow pursed his lips and then shrugged.

'Dunno just what I am, Larry, but that don't mean I can be pushed around. I aim to get along with folks where I can, but I'm the one draws the line.'

McMartin swallowed and forced a laugh. 'You sure do! Well, I better get some posts cut while you dig out the other broken ones, eh?'

Benbow smiled thinly. 'Reckon that's a good idea.'

They got along fine after that and by noon had three of the four long panels standing firmly again. The fire had burned down but the stench of charred hair and flesh was still thick on the air. Libby brought them out some sandwiches, a kerchief held to nose and mouth. She seemed pleased. 'Al's a good worker,' Larry told her. 'Knows what he's about. . . . We'll have it all repaired by sundown.'

Libby smiled at Benbow who was munching hungrily on his second cold beef sandwich. 'Glad you're settling in, Al.' Her gaze drifted off to the hills. 'I wonder how Greg and the posse are doing?'

Benbow swallowed a mouthful of bread and meat. 'If they're looking for Indians, they're wastin' their time.' She frowned, and he added, 'Whoever hit your herds were riding shod horses – and renegade bucks from a reservation so close wouldn't go on a killing spree. From what I heard in Doc Gabriel's infirmary, it seemed like cold-blooded murder of your nighthawks.'

'Well . . . we haven't had much trouble with the Indians. Occasionally, a few bucks have got drunk and raised a little hell, but nothing too serious. I'm inclined to agree with you, Al. But Sheriff Heffernan should have noticed that – he used to be a scout for the army.'

Benbow shrugged, rubbing at his head just below the wound. His head throbbed and he felt a little dizzy but he didn't want to let on. Larry was watching his every move carefully, ready to report back to old

Hec Munro. Benbow was surprised that Larry had told the girl he was a good worker.

Libby returned to the ranch house and the two men went back to mending fences. They were also to clean up the wrecked buckboard and in mid-afternoon made a bonfire out of the splintered planks and wheels and the broken fenceposts.

Benbow, raking some charred wood into the flames, glanced up through the smoke and saw Larry watching him with a puzzled expression. The man jumped guiltily, flushing.

'Something on your mind, kid?'

'I – er – was just wonderin' what it feels like. Not bein' able to remember, you know. . . .'

'Terrible, kid, just something – terrible.'

Larry waited but Benbow said no more, just wiped the grime and sweat from his face with his kerchief and then said, 'If we're all through, I'm gonna wash up in the river.'

Larry sat on the bank while Benbow stripped and scrubbed himself with a handful of sand. He noticed how tense the cowboy seemed.

'You're kinda jumpy, aren't you, Larry?'

McMartin pointed across the river. 'That's Circle G over there.'

Benbow frowned. 'Granger's place? Heffernan mentioned it.'

'Yeah – well, he's got some hardcases workin' for him.'

'So. . . ?'

'Once in a while they come and – roust us. Like if we're washin' in the river they'll come chase us out or run us around in the water, ride off with our clothes. Coupla times they beat-up on Sting Laker and Cass Doubleday.'

Benbow waded ashore, sat down on a rock to let the sun dry his lean body. 'Granger a problem?'

'That's the funny part – he don't seem to be. Sent down some men to help us out when we was short-handed one time, gave Greg some wire to string across a box canyon where we were holdin' mavericks, that sort of thing. Must be the crew themselves seem to have it in for us.'

'Trouble with them in town, too?'

Larry shrugged. 'Few brawls – but, you know, no worse'n the usual ranch rivalry, I guess. But that Jethro Caine is mighty rough. Busted a coupla arms and heads.'

'Who's he?'

'Granger's ramrod and hired gun.'

Benbow seemed to think about it and then shrugged, reaching for his clothes. 'Well, you can point out Circle G men when they're around and I'll give 'em a wide berth.'

For some reason, Larry seemed a mite disappointed.

It was dark when Greg and some of the posse rode back into the ranchyard. There were a couple of Tess Dalton's cowhands with him, as well as Heffernan who was leading a horse on a rope halter.

In the slice of yellow lamplight that spilled into the yard, Benbow saw the animal clearly.

It was an Appaloosa, with very dark hind-quarters

that allowed the signature white spots to show up clearly, like a scattering of snowflakes.

'Isn't that the horse that belongs to that Church feller – the geologist?' he asked Hec Munro, but the man only grunted.

But Heffernan had heard and put his mount across quickly, squinting down at Benbow. 'And how would you know that – Mister No-Memory?'

'Libby told me about him earlier. Still think I'm faking amnesia, Sheriff?'

'Fact is, Benbow, I dunno *what* to think about you, but I aim to solve your mystery sooner or later. I'm a patient man.'

Larry was stroking the muzzle of the Appaloosa and Benbow saw that its hide was scratched, with small twigs and leaves caught in the dirt matting its hair.

'Where you find him, Greg?' Larry asked his boss.

'Running wild in the southern pasture of Tess Dalton's place . . . seems he'd been turned loose in the brush up in the ranges but made his way down.'

Heffernan was still staring at Benbow. 'In the same area where Tess came across you. I reckon that hoss has been loose for a week or so. You wouldn't know anythin' about that, I guess.'

'You guess right, Sheriff – I've never seen the horse before.'

'Or you – don't remember,' the sheriff said flatly.

Benbow nodded. 'That's about the strength of it.'

'Wash up at the pump, Sheriff,' Greg Lacy said abruptly. 'And I'll go tell Libby to make some extra supper.'

'No luck with the rustlers?' Benbow asked, and Greg shook his head, tight-lipped.

'Must be good at hiding tracks – I hear the sheriff here used to be an Indian scout.'

'It was rainin' like the forty days and nights up there,' bristled Howie. 'You sayin' I didn't look hard enough?'

Benbow arched his eyebrows. 'Did I say anything like that?' He looked around at the others but no one made any motion that either confirmed or denied. 'Sheriff, I guess you're mighty tired and just a leetle touchy . . . I was just opining.'

'I never found no tracks because there weren't any!' the sheriff snapped, provoked into the answer by his frustration as much as Benbow's words. 'Aaah – let's go eat. My belly's restin' on my backbone. . . .'

'Don't think Howie likes you much, Benbow,' Hec Munro opined.

'Could be,' Benbow allowed, but he didn't seem worried about it.

But maybe he should have been, because Heffernan was riled at him now. Whether to shift interest from his failure to track down the rustler killers, or for some other reason, it was hard to say, but Howie Heffernan aimed to solve the mystery of this 'Al Benbow' when he got back to his office.

Previously, he had checked with Laramie and, as the description fitted pretty close, figured he was Benbow the bounty hunter, beard and all.

Now, with the man being clean-shaven, he looked different and Howie figured it wouldn't hurt any to go through his Wanted dodgers and look for a description of a fugitive or outlaw that fitted the way Benbow looked now.

He had a hunch that he might have some success. *Then* Mr No-Memory might suddenly start to make some kind of sense.

CHAPTER 7

MEDICINE MAN

The sheriff stayed overnight at the Lazy L while the other posse-men returned to town or their ranches. The rain had turned to a fading drizzle which made Heffernan curse. They might have found some tracks if it hadn't caught them in the goddamn hills!

'You tell Tess I'll need to talk with her some more and take another look around her southern pasture,' Howie Heffernan told the TD ranch hands when the posse was breaking up. 'That damn Appaloosa had to come from somewhere and it looks mighty like Ashley Church never made it to Laramie.'

Next morning, Greg Lacy sat on the porch and smoked an after-breakfast cigarette with the lawman. The sun was shining. 'Another mystery, Howie . . . Church's Appaloosa.'

Heffernan looked worried, his eyes redder than usual, and Lacy figured he hadn't slept well. 'There's somethin' queer goin' on in this valley – and it all started since that ranny Benbow turned up.'

'I dunno about that, Howie. Things were kind of tense before Benbow arrived, what with the geologist and one thing and another.'

'It's the "one thing and another" that's gotten bigger. Hell, Greg, five men dead in a couple of days! Benbow killed two of 'em and you'd think it meant no more to him than swattin' a couple of cockroaches. And them notches on his gun mean six dead men. I'd like to know who they were and just how they died.'

Lacy was sitting up straight now. 'You think he might be a gunfighter?'

'I think he's a *killer*, that's what I think – and when I can prove it, I'm gonna slap him behind bars.'

'He's good at ranch work, Libby says.'

'Well, I've known gunfighters good at a ranch job – bronc-bustin', brush-poppin', brandin', the whole works – but they hire out their gun along with their cowboyin'.'

'Hell! There's nothing in this valley that needs a hired gun on anyone's payroll!'

'Well, like I said, it can be done on the quiet. But whatever's behind this Benbow, I aim to find out.'

He heaved to his feet, tossing his cigarette butt into the yard. 'Thank Libby for a real fine meal and a good bed, too – I'll go see Tess and then head on back to town. . . .'

Lacy watched him ride away, leading the Appaloosa that Benbow had – off his own bat – currycombed and groomed last night. It sure looked a mighty fine animal.

He felt a flutter in his belly: he knew something must have happened to Church, the geologist, No man would just abandon a horse like that.

And they hadn't found his saddle or warbag, either.

When Heffernan finally got back to town just after sundown, he was plumb tuckered.

It had been a long day, starting with his questioning of Tess Dalton. He hadn't figured she would know anything about Church or the Appaloosa but the horse had been found on her land and it was a starting point for his new investigations.

The mystery of the rustler raid on Lazy L – and Circle G, if you could believe Hilt Granger, though he had really found little or no sign that it had happened – well, all that would have to wait a while. He was stymied for now, without any tracks to follow or any other clues, but he wanted this thing about Benbow cleared up, not to mention Church.

The man worked for a powerful railroad company and they wouldn't take kindly to things if something had happened to him. He would need to wire Laramie again and make sure the man hadn't arrived, but it was unlikely. He had been mighty proud of dickering with the Indians for that Appaloosa and he wouldn't just turn it loose in the brush.

Tess hadn't been able to help him and when he had asked if she thought Benbow might have had anything to with Church's disappearance, she had bristled.

'Howie, you saw the man for yourself! Saw the head wound. . . .'

'And still dunno how he got it.'

'Well, Ashley Church wouldn't have given it to him if that's what you're thinking! He wasn't a violent man and he didn't even carry a six-gun.'

'Had a saddle gun, though, a rifle. No way of tellin' what kind of bullet made Benbow's wound.'

'Oh, for heaven's sake! You're pursuing the man – surely he has enough trouble with his memory gone!'

Heffernan had scratched at his stubble that was itching. 'Be kind of convenient not to remember some things, wouldn't it? Specially disappearin' men and others dead.'

That had given her pause and she had been pretty quiet while she and one of her men rode into the hills with the sheriff, searching for sign of where the Appaloosa had come from.

They had found nothing definite but there was some distinctive hair high up near timberline, rubbed against rough bark, and they concluded the horse might have come up and over the range from the other side. Heffernan was too damn tired by that time to get excited about such a thing and he called it a day and returned to town.

He took his own mount and the Appaloosa to the livery, told the hostler to keep the horse in a corral and to make *damn* sure nothing happened to it. Going out he saw Benbow's buckskin in a stall and the livery owner confirmed the man was in town.

'Doc Gabriel had my roustabout ride out to Lazy L and tell him to come in.'

'What for?'

The livery man shrugged. 'I dunno – but there's a medicine show arrived and one of the fellers from it has been at Doc's place all day.'

Heffernan swore softly as he left. He walked down to the town square and saw the snake-oil wagon setting up in the vacant lot on the corner of South Street and the square.

He thought this show might have been here before, but wasn't sure: they all looked pretty much the same. Had a painted woman dance with a snake or something to draw the crowd. Someone else told a few jokes and maybe sang a song. Then there might be some kind of magic show and finally, the real reason they were there – a fast-talking salesman who did his best to sell their snake-oil or bear salve or some kind of foul-tasting muddy mixture that would cure anything from dandruff to smallpox if you were loco enough to believe the spiel. He looked at some of the banners they were stringing up between the two wagons. *Miracle Cure. Greatest Elixir Since God Invented Water. Men – Get Back That Special Zest For Living! (Private Consultations by the world-famous Professor Schnell).*

'Always some foreign-soundin' name,' growled Heffernan and was swinging away towards his office when he saw another banner just going up.

By popular demand! Return appearance of famous Doctor Wellington Wise, Hypnotist Extraordinaire. Forgetful? Suffer headaches? Backache? Mental Blackouts? The Incredible Dr Wise can help Y O U !

Heffernan stopped a bustling member of the medicine show troupe, a small man in a straw hat. 'Friend, who's this Doctor Wise? He got a licence to put people in a trance?'

The man looked suddenly alarmed. He shook his head quickly. 'I – I am only a temporary associate, Sheriff. Can't help you. But if you want to see the doctor, I believe he's visiting your local medico.'

Heffernan swung away, hurrying towards Doc Gabriel's.

He went straight in, hearing voices in the parlour which seemed to be very badly lit. No – only one voice, a smooth, easy-sounding voice, almost monotonous.

'Just relax – slowly – slowly – feel your limbs getting heavier, the blood draining from your head, leaving you wonderfully euphoric – floating – your entire body is – floating on a cloud. You've never felt so relaxed and at peace. Just let yourself drift – drift across the sky and feel the sun's warmth on your skin – that's it, that's it.'

Heffernan stopped in the doorway. Three people were in the room which was lit only by a single candle. Doc Gabriel sitting quietly in a corner, Al Benbow who seemed to be asleep in an easy chair, his arms dangling limply over the side, and the third man: he was slim, medium tall, dressed in frock coat and striped trousers that had seen better days. He had a large mop of unruly silver hair and, as he lifted one of Benbow's arms, let it fall limply, he glanced towards the sheriff. Heavy silver eyebrows drew together and he placed a long, arthritically deformed finger against his lips.

Gabriel waved Heffernan to the sofa irritably and the sheriff moved quietly across, frowning. The silver-haired man, whom he knew as the Amazing Doctor Wellington Wise, spoke in those dreamy dulcet tones the lawman had heard when he had entered.

'Your name is Al Benbow – would that be Alvin? Albert? Allan? Can you tell me what "Al" stands for?'

'No.'

Heffernan, seated beside Gabriel now, jumped a little as Benbow spoke, his eyes still closed, chin on his chest. The voice sounded hollow, remote.

'Well, never mind, we'll learn later, I've no doubt . . . Al . . . you're feeling very hot. The sun is beating down on you and you're thirsty. Yes! Just look at the sweat beading your face. . . . Oh, it's mighty hot out here in the desert, isn't it?'

'Damn – right. Need water . . . must have – water. . . .'

'Of course.' Wise took an empty shotglass from a table and held it to Benbow's eager lips, tilting his head back a little. 'Not too fast now. Don't drink too much at once. . . . There. Feel better?'

Benbow nodded, running a tongue over his lips. Then he lifted an arm and wiped the back of a wrist over his mouth. The sheriff straightened, snapped his head around towards Gabriel.

'Christ! He believes he had a glass of water!'

'Hush!' said Wise curtly, then turned back to Benbow. 'Now you have to push on if you're going to get across this desert by sundown.'

'So – damn – hot. . . . No food – no water. . . .'

'But you must keep going, Al! You *must*!'

'Why the hell's he tellin' him he's in a desert?'

'Because Benbow has been having nightmares of almost dying in a desert. . . . Now be quiet, Howie, or you'll spoil it all. Doctor Wise is making him regress – with luck we'll find out just what happened to him.'

Heffernan snorted derisively but he folded his arms and kept quiet.

'How you doing, Al?' Wise asked softly. 'Will you make it safely out of the desert before sundown?'

'Dunno – glare blind. . . . Thirsty.'

Wise went through the ritual of the empty glass again and Benbow nodded his thanks, again wiped a wrist over his mouth as if it was wet.

'It's all right, Al, you made it out of the desert and into green-grass country. Trees and water and—'

'Birds!' Benbow said, 'Birds in the trees – and a river. Goddamn, a *river*! I'm saved!'

'Yes, you're safe now, Al, you and your horse can drink to your hearts' content. Where did you get such a fine-looking buckskin by the way?'

Silence.

Wise frowned at Gabriel, asked the question again.

'Dunno.' Benbow's reply was curt and he was obviously tensing up. 'Hoss died in desert – not a buckskin.'

'I'd like to know how you came by the horse you're riding now, Al. And the clothes – where did you get them? You were in rags in the desert, remember? Now you have a good jacket, shirt and trousers, even a six-gun that has notches on the butt.'

Benbow shook his head. 'Not mine.'

'But it is, Al! That gun and the letter in the jacket pocket belongs to you, Al Benbow. Where did you go after you got out of the desert? You remember, don't you?'

Benbow straightened in the chair and his eyes opened although they looked a little glazed. '*Not* my gun – I don't cut notches on my guns.'

'I'm glad that you can remember that, Al.'

Gabriel and Heffernan both leaned forward, staring at him. Wise held out a hand, holding them back.

'But whose gun is it, Al? And the clothes? They're yours, aren't they?'

Benbow rubbed roughly at his forehead. 'I – dunno – got one helluva – headache . . . I. . . .'

He blinked and looked around the room startled.

Wise's lips tightened. 'Damnittohell!' he hissed. 'He's brought himself out of the trance! Just as we were getting somewhere. It must be something he *really* doesn't want to remember and his brain won't let him!'

The sheriff stood and walked across to stand by Benbow's chair where the man was trying to orientate himself.

'You were gettin' nowhere,' Howie growled at Wise. 'I recollect last time you was here you put some folks in a trance, had 'em crowin' like roosters, scamperin' round the stage on all fours, barking like dogs, lowin' like cows. You made a fool of a lot of townsfolk and now you've made a fool outa Benbow.' He grabbed Benbow by the shoulder. 'You all right, friend?'

Benbow was obviously still dazed and bewildered as he looked up into the lawman's face. He shifted his gaze to Wise and then to Gabriel. He seemed to relax some then.

'Hell, glad to see you, Doc! I – thought I was back in – that desert. . . .'

His eyes touched the silver-haired man who smiled and thrust out his right hand. 'Doctor Wellington Wise, my friend, sometime colleague of Dr Gabriel. He thought I might be able to help with your problem – the amnesia, I mean.'

Benbow shook hands indifferently.

'He can't help you, Benbow!' Heffernan said with open scepticism. 'He's a snake-oil man, from a medicine show. Puts folk into a trance so they make fools of themselves, all to sell a few bottles of "miracle" medicines that wouldn't cure a sick canary. . . .'

Benbow looked soberly at Gabriel. 'This is the man you sent for? The one with *radical* treatment?'

'Thanks a lot, Howie, for inspiring such confidence!' Gabriel snapped, tightlipped. But he forced a smile. 'We've hardly been operating under ideal conditions, Al. I can make arrangements for a better – environment – than this where Dr Wise can concentrate his powers better. I'm still convinced he can help you remember. He's had a great deal of experience in the field of fugitive memory.'

'I gave you water when you were in the desert,' Wise said, quietly smiling. 'Just now – you didn't doubt then that I could help.'

Benbow frowned and touched his mouth. 'By hell! I did have a drink of water . . . didn't I?'

They smiled at his bewilderment. Leastways, the doctors did. Heffernan's scowl only deepened.

'Tricks! All fancy damn tricks!'

'Howie, you're not helping,' Gabriel told him coldly. 'I think it would be best if you went.'

Heffernan glared around. 'Benbow, I ain't happy with you. Too many men've been killed since you showed up. *I*'m gonna look into your past and I guarantee I'll find out more than this hoaxer and his snake-oil antics!'

'I don't care who does it, as long as I find out in the end,' Benbow said, and Heffernan left as Doc Gabriel held the door open for him, stiff faced.

'Al, I'd like you to sit down and have a quiet talk with Dr Wise – I'm *sure* it'll be the best thing for you.'

'Well, I dunno, Doc. I'm obliged for what you're trying to do but – well, OK, just for a few minutes.'

Outside, just as he turned into Main, Sheriff Heffernan, still fuming, bumped into a lanky man in range clothes.

'Watch where the hell you're goin'!' the lawman growled, shoving the cowboy away roughly.

'Who the hell you shovin'? Ah! The law – might've knowed it, throwin' your weight around as usual.'

The cowboy's voice was sneering and Heffernan reached out and grabbed his arm as the man started by. 'Hold up there! We don't like troublemakers here, feller.'

'Well, I ain't here to make trouble – *feller*!' The cowboy prised Heffernan's fingers from his arm, glaring. He had a hawk-like face with a bent nose and a long jaw, now stubbled with dark beard and caked with dust.

This man had done some long, hard riding lately.

'Just why are you here? In my town, you need to have the price of a bed and breakfast – or I can give you free room and board in my lock-up for the night. And a mornin' in court afterwards.'

The lanky man seemed to calm down some now and said in a reasonable voice, 'I got some money – here, look.' He held two crumpled bills and some loose change,

Heffernan poked at it with a finger, grunted, and looked hard into the man's face.

'What's your name?'

The man hesitated, then said, 'Kip Benbow – I hear my brother Al's in town. All I want to do is see him and then I'll be on my way.'

Howie Heffernan was interested now and he started to speak but stopped when he saw someone coming through the gate in Doc Gabriel's front fence. It was Al Benbow.

'Well, there he is, friend – here comes your brother now.'

Kip Benbow turned quickly, a half-smile of welcome on his face. Then it disappeared and his jaw hardened as the man coming along the boardwalk passed through a slab of light spilling out of a barber's shop that was still open.

'What the hell is this?' Kip Benbow asked, swinging back to the lawman. 'That ain't my brother! That's Jack Brett – he's a goddamn outlaw!'

CHAPTER 8

THE BAD OLD DAYS

Kip Benbow lunged forward and the sheriff, stunned by the man's words, was a beat or two behind him as he made to grab his arm.

'Hold up!'

Kip shook off his hand and, when the lawman made another grab, slapped his arm aside with a vicious blow, hitting Heffernan on one shoulder and sending him staggering, eventually going down on one knee.

Al Benbow – or Jack Brett, according to Kip – saw the scuffle, slowed, frowning, and then he was face-to-face with Kip. The man thrust forward, snarling.

'What you done to my brother, you son of a bitch?'

Brett was taken aback, but barely had time to draw a breath before Kip Benbow hit him in the chest. He stumbled back as the man came after him, swinging.

Brett covered instinctively, ducking and weaving, catching a glimpse of Heffernan, now upright, hurrying forward, his face grim. Kip's next blow skidded along Brett's jaw and it *hurt.* Lights danced and swirled before his eyes and his lifting guard just managed to stop the following straight right. He brushed the fist aside and hit Benbow just above the belt buckle. Kip grunted and his legs wobbled as he sagged in the middle, gagging for air. Heffernan had arrived and tried to get between the men. He caught a left hook on one ear from Brett and it staggered him. The man shoved him aside without really noticing him, straight-armed Kip as he began to unbend, jarring the man's head on his shoulders. Benbow waved his arms for balance and Jack Brett – if that was his name – followed swiftly, shouldering the dazed lawman aside, fists swinging. Benbow floundered into a fence and Brett crowded him, beating a tattoo of blows from his belt line to his throat. Benbow started to fall to one side, twisting, lifting an arm instinctively for protection.

Brett ducked under and drove three straight rights into his face like the multiple strikes of a diamondback, brought over his left, which hit Benbow's jaw with a loud crack. Kip corkscrewed all the way round and hung over the fence, arms dangling loosely, hat falling off.

Brett came around in a blur as iron fingers dug into his shoulder. Sheriff Howie Heffernan was snarling, his face having a lopsided look now, as he brought up his six-gun. Then the lawman sucked in a sharp, hissing breath and lifted to his toes as a gun barrel rammed into his midriff and Brett said, 'Leave it, Sheriff!'

Heffernan was shocked at the speed of the draw and immediate threat that meant certain death if he was stupid enough to continue. He didn't even recall letting his gun fall but it dropped on to his toe and he jumped back, howling, feeling mighty foolish.

A small crowd had gathered now as the scuffle had taken place near the intersection with Main. They stared at Brett, the man they still knew as Al Benbow, and then at Kip Benbow, moaning and writhing as he slowly regained his senses.

Brett held his gun with the hammer spur under his thumb, glanced at Kip, then set his gaze on the sheriff.

'You saw that.' He gestured towards Benbow who was straightening groggily. 'He walked right up to me and started swinging.'

Howie was rubbing at his throbbing ear, wary of the Colt covering him. 'He's Kip Benbow.' He let that sink in for a moment, then added, 'Says you ain't his brother – that you're an outlaw named Jack Brett.'

The accused man frowned in silence, then slowly shook his head. 'Doesn't mean a thing to me, Sheriff.'

Heffernan smiled crookedly. 'Well, I sure wouldn't expect you to admit to bein' an outlaw, but it could explain why you claim you don't remember who you are.'

Jack Brett smiled, too. 'You got a devious mind, Howie! But, yeah, I can see how you might think that way. Only I'm not fooling. I don't remember who I am. Tess Dalton fitted me up with the name Al Benbow because of that letter in my jacket pocket –

at the time, it was as good a name as any for me. Same as Jack Brett is now.'

'You mightn't think that if I find a dodger on you.'

'You got a point there.' Brett took a step back and to one side as, out of the corner of his eye, he saw Benbow lunging towards him, lifting a Colt ready to gunwhip him to the ground.

He swung his own revolver, hitting Benbow's forearm, and making the man stumble. A second blow tore the gun from Benbow's hand and Kip nursed his aching arm, swearing.

The sheriff grabbed at his fallen gun but Brett's weapon was covering him again, hammer cocked, and the lawman let his Colt stay put and straightened slowly, arms out from his sides.

'You move fast, mister!'

Brett said nothing. People were coming out of houses in the short street, hanging over fences. A gate hinge squealed and suddenly the silver-haired Wellington Wise was standing beside Brett, taking his arm.

'Let go, Doc!'

Startled at the cold, menacing words, Wise released the arm, stepped back. 'I heard! This man knows you! He says your name is Jack Brett! Now is the time to follow through, don't you see? I don't know about the mix-up with the Benbow name, but this time you have your real name to think about! If I can put you under again there's a mighty good chance you'll remember the things you've been trying to!'

Brett frowned and Heffernan looked from him to

the medicine-show man. 'I might be interested in that.'

'Thought you were an unrepentant sceptic, Sheriff.'

Heffernan sighed. 'This is such a damn Irish stew of things, I'm about willin' to try anythin'. . . . How about you?' He looked at Brett and the man hesitated, then nodded curtly, but he kept an eye on Benbow.

'Yeah, you better keep watchin' me!' Kip Benbow growled. 'You been ridin' my brother's buckskin and you're wearin' his jacket . . . I want to know what you've done to him!'

'He had a letter on him,' Heffernan said slowly. 'Woman who found Brett naturally assumed it was addressed to him.' The sheriff obviously liked the idea of Brett being an outlaw.

Benbow nodded, still watching Brett. 'Yeah – I wrote Al, askin' for five hundred bucks.'

'Gamblin' debt, I believe,' put in the sheriff.

'That's right – I guess it's my weakness.'

'So is shootin' gamblers from what I hear. Latest count's three – am I right?'

Benbow stiffened. 'They was all fair and square shoot-outs, ask any of the lawmen in the towns where they happened. But Al's a bounty hunter. He's always took care of me. He didn't have five hundred bucks, but he said he'd just seen a new dodger on some outlaw named Jack Brett who had a thousand or so bounty on him. He knew where he was and aimed to go after him, collect, and then send me the money – I ain't heard from him for weeks so I figured to come up and see for myself if everythin' was OK.' He glared again at Brett. 'But I'm thinkin' this snake has killed Al and took his hoss and clothes and is usin' his name to dodge the law!'

'You ain't as dumb as you try to sound, Benbow,' Heffernan said sardonically. 'Same thoughts just hit me – you got anythin' to add, Brett?'

'No – Brett is as good a name as any as far as I'm concerned. It hasn't triggered anything in my memory—'

'Not that you're aware of!' Wellington Wise put in swiftly. He appealed to Heffernan. 'Sheriff – please. This is the opportunity to unlock this man's clouded memory. I know you think I'm a charlatan and use trickery and I admit to using some tricks in the medicine show – but *I am a doctor qualified in what is becoming known in Europe as hypnotherapy* – the use of hypnosis to unlock painful or hidden memory in the human mind . . . Doctor Gabriel knows my background and will vouch for me.

'I'll try it, Doc,' Brett said, holding up a hand as Heffernan made to speak. 'It's my head, Sheriff. And I need to know who I am and what I've been doing. Sure, I know you want to lock me up and start wading through a heap of Wanted dodgers, but you can still do that after the – whatever it is he called it.'

'Hypnotherapy. What d'you say, Sheriff? I have no objection to your sitting-in but I must insist that you refrain from commenting aloud. I require total silence.

'C'mon, Heffernan,' growled Benbow. 'I want to know what happened to Al – I don't believe this ranny's really forgotten what he did, but I don't aim to let him out of my sight, neither.'

Heffernan still hesitated, finally nodded curtly. 'We'll try it – but I warn you, Brett, I'll be sittin' with my gun in my hand!'

Wellington Wise threw up his hands but realized he wasn't going to get a better deal.

The small group pushed through the crowd and started back towards Doc Gabriel's house.

He didn't know the man's name and was pretty sure he had never seen him before, but it was obvious he was on the prod.

He came in through the batwings, a short silhouette against the high-noon glare of Main Street, hat pushed back as he squinted myopically around the smoke-hazed bar room. Jack Brett was downing his second beer at the bar, thinking he had better clear town as soon as he got enough grub to fill his saddle-bags, and an extra canteen of water for the desert crossing. He hoped anyone along his backtrail would decide that no one but a crazy man would tackle that Saltlick Desert.

He smacked his lips, set down the glass and wiped his wrist across his mouth as he looked around casually. It seemed casual but it was his usual check that there was no trouble brewing before he made his exit.

Then he saw the man in the batwings.

He paused in the sweep of his gaze, feeling a slight lurch: was this someone who had his name on their list to gun down? A lawman from some other county throwing protocol aside just so he could get a crack at Brett?

He hadn't decided when the short man lifted an arm, his left, finger rigid as it nailed Brett to the bar. He started forward determinedly and his voice was mellow and smooth although he looked like he had ridden hard and far.

'You – Brett!'

As he spat the name his right hand swept up his six-gun and men dived for cover. Brett merely stepped quickly to one side, his own gun whipping up as he did so. His Colt blasted a fraction of a second before the other's gun and the short man staggered, his bullet blasting splinters from the bar front. Brett was rolling across the floor by that time down in the wet sawdust. He rammed his elbow in deep and his arm steadied as he triggered again. The bullet seemed to lift the short man completely off his feet and he crashed into the wall beside the batwings and slid down, tumbling on to his face. He had dropped his own gun and he didn't make any move now, except to twitch a little.

Brett climbed slowly to his feet, smoking pistol still pointing at the downed man. He glanced at a man in a frock coat standing rigidly a few feet from the sprawled gunman.

'Check him,' Brett said, and moved slowly, watching warily as the frock-coated man knelt and felt for the neck pulse.

He shook his head. 'Dead.'

'You found that pulse mighty quick, mister!'

'No pulse to find – but I know where to look. I'm the local doctor.'

Brett sighed. 'Then I guess I got to take your word

for it.' He raked his hard eyes around the room where no one seemed in a hurry to make any kind of a move, even to leave the saloon. 'He called me out – you all saw that.' No one answered and Brett frowned. He raised his voice. 'You all saw that! He called me!'

The doctor cleared his throat. 'I more or less followed that man in here, sir, and all I heard was him call a name – Brett, I believe.'

'That's my name, Doc, but he was going for his gun as he said it.'

There was a ripple of a murmur then and Brett frowned more deeply, looked around sharply. 'What's wrong?'

The barkeep cleared his throat. 'Mister – I – I seen it all and – well, you drew first.'

Others backed up the barkeep and Brett swore softly.

'I got my gun out first because I was faster! He made the first move, but I beat him to the draw. . . .'

His words trailed off as he saw bewilderment and plain scepticism on the faces of the crowd. Without any more hesitation, Brett backed to the side door, covering the tense drinkers, and stepped swiftly out into the alley.

No time to replenish his dwindling supplies of food and water now: he had to clear town in a hurry. Those men in there would tell it the way they saw it to the law and that would mean a posse and pursuit – as if he didn't have enough trouble with the kin of that irascible old man who had tried to cut him in two with a shotgun out at the waterhole somewhere to the south of this dump, aiming to take his dun horse and the spare roan. There were no witnesses to prove he had gotten his gun out and blasting before the murderous old bastard could jerk the scatter-gun's triggers, so he had lit-out and halfway here had learned the dead man's kinfolk were tracking him, out for revenge.

He'd waylaid them, stripped them of guns and boots and set their mounts loose miles from where he had left them. He figured he would have time to get supplies here before he made for the Saltlick. But he had to stop for a cold beer first! *Damn fool!* The temptation to taste icy-cold beer sliding down his gullet before committing himself to the desert had been too much.

Now there was another dead man chalked up to him and no doubt a worthwhile bounty would be posted against his name.

Goddamn the luck!

But Brett wasn't the kind to waste too much time on self-recrimination. He had to get out of here – and fast.

There were many trails in every direction of the compass leading out of that town and he laid tracks on most of them before making for the barren range that would take him to the desert. It was a long time since he had made a real desert crossing but he had done it before several times, going where only lizards and Indians went and making it. He actually had a small reputation in Arizona for being the only white man to make it alive across the desert called Hades' Dinner Table.

But it had all cost him time, laying the false tracks, and he picked up a hint from a lone settler where he had stopped in the hope of replenishing his grub – and hadn't – that there was a bounty hunter looking for him.

'A thousand bucks on this Brett's head now, they say,' the settler had told him, not recognizing him for his beard was heavy by now and his clothes worn and ragged.

He had told the man his name was Jackson.

So Brett had left with a full canteen at least and made a roundabout way to the edge of the desert.

There had been enough of a dust cloud behind him the next morning to make his belly lurch: it was too big for a lone rider. But a small, hard-riding posse would lift that much dust, he figured.

There were pressures from many directions now and he was tired, unable to grab sufficient rest. He could go for a few days without sleep but his main concern was that he would grow careless, not cover his tracks as well as he should, and then they would close in – if there was a 'dead-or-alive' tag to the bounty, he knew which one the posse men would choose.

For a time he thought he had shaken them, but he had run the roan ragged and lost it in a river crossing. Lucky he had his gear on the dun. He raced for the shortcut through the cutting that would lead him to the desert trail.

Nope! No sign of the dust cloud! He felt elated as he cut down the steep slope and made his way up the dry riverbed to the entrance of the narrow cutting. It was rugged going and the horse had to pick its way carefully.

Then halfway through the cutting, with the slanting, narrow walls seeming to topple in towards him, a rifle crashed, the whiplashing shot slapping back and forth in ear-drumming echoes. The dun swerved a little, grunted, as it stepped into a rocky patch and he heard a dull sound just behind his left hip. He thought the bullet had bored into the thick leather and wooden frame of the saddle. He spurred the dun forward and it wasn't until he had travelled miles into the desert that the horse started to falter – and finally died under him.

He crashed face first into the sand and spat and choked as he rolled away from the thrashing carcass, swearing when he noticed his canteen and rifle were on the underside of the animal. At least the bushwhacker hadn't yet caught up with him. There had only been that one shot and then he had managed to get under the overhang until he had cleared the cutting. That was when he had realized the gunman couldn't find a way down this side and would have to ride back over the mountain before he gained entrance to the cutting.

With a little luck, he might make it to the sandhill country by sundown and he could lose any pursuit during the cold dark hours of the desert night.

The desert crossing was a nightmare. And just when he thought it was going to end, when his tongue was swollen in his throat, his skin was peeling off his face and the backs of his hands were red-raw and stinging with sunburn, his head throbbing like a Comanche drum, it took a new turn.

He was lying face down on the steep slope of a high dune with sand sliding down and slowly burying his head and shoulders. He had enough reason left to lift his head and shake it free of the engulfing sand. But he lost his grip and his whole body began to slide away. His hands clawed but the sand was fluid and it passed between his fingers like water. His boots dug in but they, too, just kept sliding.

It occurred to his sun-tortured brain that when he reached the bottom, he would have no strength left and the tons of moving sand would simply continue to keep coming and pile up and over his body, burying him feet deep before it finally stopped. And by that time he wouldn't care whether it stopped or not because his lungs would be full of sand and alkali. . . .

So this is where and how it ends . . . end of the trail for a 'gunfighter'. Hell, everyone seemed convinced he was out to take on the world and spit in the face of the devil . . . now he couldn't even raise enough saliva to dribble from his swollen, split lips, let alone spit. . . .

Then something grabbed him by the ankle and he gave a choked, gagging cry, feeling the bitter, hot alkali-laced sand filling his mouth. He choked and began to cough and hawk. The thing grabbing his ankle was relentless, dragging him backwards, driving more sand up his nostrils. He flailed weakly, tried to twist, kick his leg free. But something gripped that leg, too, and heaved, and he was finally pulled free of the moving sand, felt the now blessed heat of the scorching sun on his abraded flesh. But he was choking. Sand and grit behind his nose, clogging his throat, searing his eyes . . . not enough clearance in his mouth to draw in air. . . .

Blackness shot through with flames reached for him and when the racking coughing didn't provide any relief, he felt himself going and he thought: *To hell with it! Just go with it to wherever it ends.* He knew it would be Hell but what did that matter now? Nothing mattered – just get it over with and—

Tepid water splashed into his face, washing out his eyes, fingers reached into his mouth and cleared it of sand and more water almost choked him.

He had ten minutes of convulsive, pain-stabbing agony and came to his senses leaning on one elbow, head hanging, thick, gritty saliva stretching from his mouth to the sand where he lay, his lungs feeling as if they had been torn out and the cavity filled with hot stones. His throat was aflame. He couldn't see properly.

But he knew something that sent a surge of relief through him: He didn't know how or why, but he was still alive!

Alive!

CHAPTER 9

THE BAD OLD DAYS – II

It was dark when he came round properly.

There was a small camp-fire and he felt that he was leaning his back against a rock. He tried to rub at his face with his right hand but found he couldn't move it.

Something was holding his wrist, tight and cold and hard – and hurting. He actually jumped when he looked down and saw the metal of a set of handcuffs, reflecting the glow of the small camp-fire. One manacle round his wrist, the other locked around the remains of a branch of a dead tree, the log having been turned so that the stub dug deeply into the ground, effectively kept him anchored. His only area of movement was no more than the distance he could stretch his arm. And it hurt to pull too tight.

'Just tell me what you want,' a voice said and Brett

snapped up his head, 'and I'll get it for you.'

There was a man hunkering down by the fire, eating from a tin plate. Looked like beans and Brett's belly rumbled. He gave the short chain on the handcuffs another tug.

'How about the key?'

The man laughed. 'I guess you're feelin' better.'

'Lawman?' Brett asked hoarsely, grimacing at the pain in his throat. The inside of his mouth felt raw, gritty, but he managed to find enough spittle to fire it over his lips. It sizzled against a glowing twig.

The man shook his head. 'Not law – bounty hunter.'

'Hell! How'd you get on to me so fast? I thought that desert'd throw any pursuit.'

The man chuckled. He stood, sauntered over, wiping his hands on his corduroy trousers. He sat on the log that held Brett prisoner, started to roll a cigarette.

'You threw the posse, but that sheriff was a dumbass, anyway. Couldn't find his own nose to blow it if he had a cold. But I did me a little research on you, Brett. You been ridin' the edge of the law for a long time. Been smart – or lucky – enough not to get caught for anythin' too serious. Mostly you kept one jump ahead of the men with tin stars because you studied the country where you'd have to make a run for it. Happened to see a note that you were the only white man ever to make it across Hades' Dinner Table desert in Arizona . . . no mean feat, *amigo*! Seen where you'd made a few other desert crossin's, too, and I said to myself, this man *likes* deserts! If he pulls a job somewhere and runs, he'll make for the closest desert. You can bet that stupid sheriff never even figured you'd try for the old Saltlick, but I played me a hunch, worked out the trail you'd need to take, and set myself up above that cuttin'.'

He paused while he lit his cigarette, his face in the flare of the match scowling a little. It was wolfish and bearded. 'Caught myself out and couldn't get down fast enough to reach you before you got into the desert proper, but caught up with you finally while you were tryin' to climb the big sandhill. You were mighty close to croakin' it when I got to you.'

Brett nodded slowly. 'I remember – you pulled me out from under that sliding sand. Must've been risky. I'm obliged, whoever-you-are.'

'Al Benbow . . . you've likely heard of me?' There was a touch of cockiness in the question.

Brett thought and shrugged. 'Seems I know the name. Make a business of bounty hunting?'

Benbow nodded, turned so Brett could see the holstered Colt with the notches carved into the wooden butt.

'It *is* my business – six men so far – six *dead* men.'

Brett stiffened. 'You gonna take me in dead?'

'Now why would I save your neck just to kill you?'

Jack Brett frowned. Benbow chuckled at his puzzlement.

'Most Wanted dodgers say dead or alive – but yours pays more to bring you in alive. . . . Now how about that?'

'I don't savvy it. . . .'

'I didn't at first, either. But seems you been a

naughty boy and robbed a train down in Socorro. Strong-box went missin', of course, and there was somethin' else important in there besides the couple of thousand in coins you got. Papers of some sort?'

Brett kept his face blank, as if he was trying to remember just what was supposed to have been in that box besides the payroll for the silver mine.

'Don't matter – thing is, the railroad's bein' sued by the mine because of these papers, whatever they are, and so the railroad wants you brought in alive so you can tell 'em what happened or lead 'em to where the papers are now.' Benbow drew deeply on his cigarette, let the smoke trickle out of mouth and nostrils. 'They won't pay nothin' for you dead. Law will, but a measly couple of hundred. Alive, I can get a thousand from the railroad—'

'The railroad sounds a better deal, all right.'

Benbow laughed. 'Yeah, sure! From your point of view, well as mine – but I need that thousand. Half of it, leastways; young brother needs the rest in a hurry – but that makes no nevermind now. We're halfway across the dunes here and I reckon I can make it to the mountains by sundown tomorrow. Then we'll find a town with a telegraph and a railroad and I'm on my way to pickin' up the bounty.'

'Well, I tell you now, I dumped that box after I took the coins. Never checked out any papers. They could be blowing all over New Mexico by now. I just needed the cash.'

Benbow shrugged. 'No skin off my nose, feller – I just take you in and collect. What happens after that just don't interest me.'

Benbow dumped some beans from a can on to a tin platter and brought it to Brett with a fork. He ate hungrily, although the beans were stone cold. The bounty hunter set some coffee brewing and while it was making, went to tend to his horse, a fine-looking buckskin.

'Damn nice horse,' Brett opined.

'You bet – gonna have to carry us both now.'

Benbow slapped a hand against his gun butt. 'Some of these gents helped pay for him. Didn't really want to take him out into that desert but he was just fine.' He patted the horse affectionately. 'Just fine. . . .'

He checked the hobbles one more time and then came back to the fire, poured two mugs of coffee and set one down where Brett could reach it. It was too hot to drink yet but Brett set it on the log near his face and blew on it from time to time, the aroma tantalizing his raw taste buds.

Benbow hunkered down, sipping slowly but constantly, the heat apparently not bothering him. He had finished before Brett could even begin sipping his own drink. The bounty hunter stood, stretched, took an old magazine from a saddle-bag.

'Gotta go see a man about a dog,' he murmured, starting for some rocks. 'Don't go 'way!'

He laughed and Brett curled a lip as the man unbuckled his trousers, slid them down and squatted amongst the rocks. Brett looked up at the stars. He could see pretty good now. The stars blazed, blue-white and brilliant. A sliver of moon edged a cloud with silver. The desert night was throbbing with silence. . . .

Until a gunshot shattered it.

A gunshot followed by a choking cry of fear.

Brett snapped his head around. Benbow was jerking to his feet, awkwardly holding his trousers at his waist with fingers that also held his smoking Colt. His other hand was clamped to his neck and he stumbled out of the rocks, floundered his way across in Brett's direction and fell to hands and knees.

'Snake!' he croaked hoarsely. 'Musta been coiled up on a rock – level with my face!'

'Judas! Where'd he get you?' Brett was drawing up his legs now, having no wish to have a riled-up rattlesnake slithering amongst the rocks while he was cuffed to this log.

'Neck. Got me in . . . the . . . neck. . . . Oh, Christ!'

Brett froze: he had never heard a note of such utter terror come from any human being. Benbow's eyes were bulging. His mouth was working and there seemed to be a lot of saliva there now, dribbling from his beard. He was blinking, shaking his head, reaching out a hand to some being Brett couldn't see. The man had dropped his hand from his neck and Brett saw the two big beads of blood and the trickles beneath the wound, right beside the thick artery.

Al Benbow was a dead man.

All he had to do was lie down. . . .

Benbow began to twist and shudder, moaning.

But Jack Brett was anchored by locked handcuffs – to a log that must weigh 700 pounds.

And he didn't yet know if Benbow had killed the snake with his one shot, or whether it was still slithering about amongst the rocks . . . maybe making its way towards him right now.

Frantically, he yanked at the handcuffs, the short chain snapping tight, but the log didn't budge a fraction of an inch. The metal cuff cut into his wrist, tearing the skin with a burning feeling.

He fought rising panic: hell, he had killed a hundred snakes in his time. Used to pick them up by hand when he was a kid in the Texas swamps around Matagorda. *Calm down!* His heart was hammering against his ribs: he felt as if it would burst out of his chest. Blood pounded in his head. He broke out in a cold sweat and he recognized that rising panic was claiming his body.

'*No*!' he shouted aloud, the sound of his voice startling him. Then he twisted from the waist up as something scraped and rattled in under the log. His breath burst from him when he saw it was a curious lizard poking its head out.

Calm down! he told himself again, took several deep breaths and, although they made him cough rackingly, he did feel better afterwards. What he had to do was get the handcuff key: it ought to be in one of the pockets of Benbow's jacket or his shirt.

But first he had to reach the man's body which had finally stopped twitching and was slumped at a contorted angle from the final convulsion. It sure wasn't pretty dying from a rattlesnake bite, Brett allowed. He tried various positions in an attempt to move the log a few inches closer to Benbow but nothing worked. All it did was make his wrist bleed and the sweat flooded his lean body, soaking his ragged clothes.

In the end, he gritted his teeth, stretched out his arm and the handcuff chain to its limit, reached with his other arm towards Benbow's body. His fingertips just brushed the cloth of the corduroy jacket. His nails were horny but worn down and he couldn't manage to catch any of the threads. He started to cuss but stopped, saving his breath, trying to keep his mind off the snake and where it might be – or if there was more than one.

He forced such thoughts from his mind, writhed around and jumped when something clattered. It was only the fork on the tin platter with the remains of the beans . . . *the fork!*

He twisted and got the sauce-slippery handle in his left hand, stretched his arm again, clenching his teeth against the pain in his right wrist. He took as firm a grip as he could on the fork, lunged towards Benbow and stabbed with the tines.

He cried out loud, thinking he had broken his wrist when the handcuffs snapped taut and the metal ring actually slid over his sweat-slippery wrist bone – but it would never come free of the hand, of course. Not without unlocking.

The fork had caught in the coat and he carefully tugged it towards him. There was some slack and one flap was within reach. He dropped the fork, grabbed a fistful of cloth and pulled.

Stitches popped rapidly and the coat tail began to tear free without moving Benbow, the man's dead weight actually helping the snapping of the thread.

Brett paused, panting. If he kept pulling, the stitches would break one by one on the seams and he would end up with a useless part of the coat and nothing more. But when he yanked one more time, the motion moved Benbow's left arm and it flopped within reach across the back of his aching hand.

He took the dead man's limp hand, locked his left around the man's wrist and heaved with a roaring effort.

The body tumbled towards him and fell across his lower legs.

Brett sat there gasping for breath, chest afire, throat raw, senses spinning. But he managed to force a laugh.

Now every part of Benbow was in reach. All he had to do was search the body and locate the handcuff key. And hope the goddamn rattlesnake didn't come for him in the meantime!

But he found it dead, head shattered by the bullet.

After burying Benbow amongst the rocks, Brett stripped off his rags of clothing and dressed in the ones he had taken from Benbow's body and the man's saddle-bags. They fitted well enough and he was glad of the corduroy jacket in the cool nights. He had found the letter Benbow had mentioned from his young brother, Kip. He had been going to screw it up and throw it away, but decided to keep it with him. It could act as identification if he felt the need to change his name.

Having lost his own six-gun in the sand slide, he strapped on Benbow's, with its six notches.

Thinking like a true outlaw, he decided to head north. If anyone should ask, he had spent too many years in the south. It was time he took a look at the new wide-open frontier up there in the Big Sky country. Make a new start. . . ? Well, the old time-worn phrase he had heard many a time over the years just might hold some hope: it always sounded good. And he had his story down pat.

Trouble seemed to follow him wherever he went but he was into his thirties now and it was time to start something new. He knew cattle and had pretty good know-how with horses. He ought to find work easy enough and then, after he had a small nest-egg – well, who knew? Land was cheap in wide-open country.

That sounded pretty good to him.

Many a man, weary of riding the owlhoot trail, had started out with good intentions and when the hard-earned money didn't come in fast enough, the temptation to pull one last job usually was too much to pass up. And, instead of a small cabin in forty acres with a few cows, most men ended up in a cell, eight by ten – or in the ground, six feet under.

But folk would see it wasn't going to happen to him. He could be stubborn and apply himself and put up with all kinds of hardships once he made up his mind, so. . . .

He rode into Wyoming, stopped off in Cheyenne, and right away found himself up to his neck in trouble the very first day.

Some slit-eyed son of a bitch took a fancy to the buckskin and tried to steal it while Brett was having a drink in a saloon. A cowboy Brett had bought a beer for and given a cigarette, came bursting in from the privy alley.

'Mister! Arch Hayes has had enough booze to turn him mean again, and he's tryin' to steal your hoss!'

Brett whirled immediately and started for the batwings. The cowboy called after him, 'Arch is hell with a six-gun, *amigo*!'

Brett was through the batwings by then and saw a big man with long hair and wild, drink-reddened eyes, fighting the buckskin, yanking on the reins and sawing the bit across the mouth as he tried to get a boot in the stirrup. The horse snorted and whinnied and kept turning. Arch Hayes, swearing as he stumbled, went down to his knees and was dragged into the gutter.

He roared to his feet, yanking his gun now. 'You goddamn jughead! I'll blow your eyes out!'

Brett drew and fired in one blurred movement and Hayes staggered, spinning, looking shocked as he turned his wild eyes on to the man with the smoking gun on the boardwalk. His mouth worked and he brought his gun around.

Brett shot him again and Hayes sat down heavily, hands in his lap, watching the blood drip from his chest wound on to his grubby trousers. He looked up, puzzled, then fell back.

Men were running up and coming out of the saloon. A neat-looking man with a polished brass star on his vest pushed to the fore, very sure of himself, even though he wasn't packing any guns. 'I better take that gun, cowboy.'

'You better not try,' Brett told him, and the man stiffened.

'Mister, I'm Sheriff Blaine McCall – I run a tight

town, don't even need guns to keep it that way – so don't mess with me! Maybe you've heard of me?'

'Dunno as I have, but I don't care if you're Brimstone Bob from the Bible Belt, that son of a bitch was trying to steal my horse and getting ready to shoot it.'

'You could've called to him!'

Brett snorted and a lot of the crowd laughed derisively, too. 'That was Arch Hayes! Hell, I heard tell of him down in Colorado. Drunk, bully, hoss-thief, rustler – what you doing letting a skunk like that run round loose, Sheriff?'

McCall flushed and his face was ugly. 'Get outa my town, mister! And I mean right now!'

Brett nodded slowly. 'I'll do that. And I won't be back if I can help it either.'

'What's your name?' snapped the lawman.

Brett hesitated, then told him defiantly as he caught the buckskin's bridle, soothed it and swung up into leather. 'You've got no dodgers on me.'

'Git, damn you!'

Brett turned the buckskin and rode away at an angle, watching the angry sheriff. Some of the townsfolk called out he'd done Cheyenne a good deed by killing Arch Hayes.

'He better ride far and fast,' opined a man at the saloon batwings.

'He asked about Laramie,' said the cowboy who had warned Brett about the horse-thief. 'Might be far enough.'

'Well, McCall will make it hard for him if he can.'

And Sheriff Blaine McCall tried to do just that. He

went to the telegraph office and wrote out a message, thrusting it at the waiting agent.

'Send that right now.'

The man nodded, used to Blaine's ill-mannered and bossy ways. He tapped out the messaage to Hilton Granger, Circle G ranch, Lander, Wind River County, Wyoming.

GUNFIGHTER HEADING YOUR WAY. NAME OF BRETT. MIGHT BE MAN YOU EXPECT. REGARDS BLAINE MCCALL.

The message meant nothing to the telegraphist but it obviously did to the sheriff. The lawman tossed the man a coin and went out whistling.

That ought to fix that hardcase's wagon for him!

CHAPTER 10

WIND RIVER

'Hold it!'

Sheriff Howie Heffernan had been quiet all through the hypnosis session with the man now called Jack Brett. It had been hard, mighty hard, but Doc Gabriel sitting beside the lawman had sensed just when Heffernan was about to make an outburst, held his arm firmly and shook his head emphatically.

Now, Heffernan could contain his silence no longer.

It was past one o'clock and they were all tired, not the least Jack Brett himself. He still looked relaxed in his chair, eyes closed, hands folded on his chest, feet up and head back. But he was frowning a little now, his head moved and an unintelligible sound came from somewhere deep in his throat.

Wellington Wise, sitting close to Brett's chair, with a notebook, looked sharply at Heffernan. 'Quiet, please! This is going very well and if we interrupt it now—'

'You better interrupt it now!' Heffernan snapped, standing, and both medical men sighed, seeing there was no stopping the man now. He glared at the medicos and pointed a finger at Brett whose eyes were still closed but there was some activity now behind the lids. Previously, during his story, his eyeballs had remained still. Wise recognized the signs.

'Dammit, Sheriff, he's disturbed now! He could even wake up!' He spoke in a hoarse, censuring voice.

'I hope so.'

'Just what's the problem, Howie?' Gabriel asked mildly, but he, too, was annoyed.

'Brett – or whatever his name is – is talkin' well, non-stop, like someone opened a gate in a dam wall and it's all rushin' out.'

'That's *exactly* what I wanted to achieve!' Wise growled.

'Yeah, yeah – but I'm interested in details. Some early-on, but the one that bothers me now is – *how did he know that Sheriff McCall sent a wire to Hilt Granger? And what was in it?*'

The two medicos slowly looked at each other. Wise cleared his throat eventually.

'A – good point, Sheriff. But couldn't it have waited until he told the rest of his story?'

'No. Because I think he's only tellin' us what he wants us to know. He's holdin' somethin' back – I don't even reckon he's in the trance you say he is.'

'Oh, I can assure you he is – I've put hundreds of people under hypnosis and I can tell readily if someone is faking.'

Heffernan shrugged. 'Still don't explain how he could know about that telegraph Blaine McCall sent from Cheyenne. Even if he hung around long enough to see McCall go into the telegraph office, he couldn't know who it was sent to or what was in it.'

'The sheriff makes a good point, Wellington,' said Gabriel softly.

Wise was willing to accept that but he was deeply puzzled – until Brett suddenly yawned aloud, stretched his arms and slowly swung his legs over the side of the tilted easy chair. He rubbed hard at his eyes and looked around at the three men.

'Told you he wasn't in any trance!'

'I stand by what I said – he was under my control. But you've broken the mood, damnit!'

Brett flicked his eyes from one man to the other.

'This will be twice he's come out of your *control*, Wise,' Heffernan said tightly. 'I still say it's all been a trick.'

'No – it's possible for patients to bring themselves out of hypnosis. They might be approaching some part of their story they don't wish to confront, or they may've been under only to a shallow degree. Their body may tell them they have had enough rest, even, and they wake up as if from a deep, relaxing sleep.'

Brett yawned again. 'That's how I feel. What's the trouble?'

Heffernan spoke up at once, playing his trump card about the telegram. Brett frowned, as if trying to recall the story he had been telling.

'McCall's telegraph message to Granger at Circle G?'

Heffernan was looking smug. 'Yeah. How'd you know about it? Or – *what was in it?*'

'I saw it on Granger's desk and read it.'

That stunned all three of the men. Heffernan looked suspicious. 'How come?'

Brett shrugged. 'I rode out to Circle G and asked for a job. The message form was lying on his desk. He saw me looking at it and covered it up with a ledger. Told me he didn't need any extra hands.'

'Why would he have been expectin' you?'

'He wasn't – I guess McCall got that wrong.'

Heffernan turned at a small sound from Wellington Wise, saw the man studying his notebook, looking concerned.

'What is it, Wise?'

'Er – nothing – I was just checking the wording of that telegram. . . .'

'No – somethin's throwed you! What is it? C'mon! I'm tired and I've had enough of your hocus-pocus for the night.'

Still Wise hesitated and then looked directly at Brett. 'I . . . feel . . . you may be concealing something, Mr Brett. Your story jumps from place to place. There are details you've left out— No, wait, please! It's not just a matter of skipping over things, because when someone is under hypnosis and they begin a story, they inevitably fill in the most mundane details – like washing their neck, or rolling a cigarette, gathering twigs for a fire, those kind of things. Over the years I've learned to ignore them and live with them . . . but there are few such details in your story. Have you ever been under hypnosis before?'

Brett shook his head, definitely. 'Only earlier on with you.'

'Well, your story sounds almost – rehearsed.'

'It's the same feelin' I got, Wise!' Heffernan said with an edge of excitement in his voice. 'He's holdin' somethin' back! Coverin'-up with a pack of lies.'

Brett shook his head again. 'Not that I know of – I can recollect what I was telling you and my heart's racing, because I can remember way back to that shoot-out before I crossed the desert.'

'That was where I had you start,' Wise said. 'Perhaps I should've taken you further back and built up to these things gradually. . . .'

'I can't remember before that bar-room fracas,' Brett said flatly.

'Can't – or don't want to?' asked Heffernan.

Brett lifted his gaze to the lawman. 'Right now I can't remember, Sheriff. You'll just have to accept that.'

Heffernan's mouth tightened. 'If you think you're gonna get out of it that easy, you're mistaken! By your own admission, you're a wanted man. I'll have a dodger on it somewhere and now I know the name and you've shaved off that beard, I'll find it.' He rammed a finger through the air in Brett's direction. 'And when I do, I'll throw you in the cells.'

Brett looked a little worried, glanced at Wise who said, 'I could try to take you back further, but I wouldn't like to do it right now. You've been under twice today and you should have a rest. Maybe in twenty-four hours. If you're agreeable, of course.'

'Ask me in twenty-four hours.' Brett stood. 'I'm

damn tired. Doc, is that bed still spare in your infirmary? Just for tonight? I'll head back to Lacy's in the morning.'

'Of course.'

'Wait up!' Heffernan grabbed Brett's arm as he made to leave. 'You ain't finished your story – or you gonna claim you don't recollect any more?'

'Now, just a minute, Sheriff, it's prudent to end this for now and—'

Heffernan ignored Wise, looking hard into Brett's face. 'Well?'

Brett shrugged. 'I can recollect something – I rode out of Circle G and took the Wind River trail. Granger suggested it, matter of fact. Said it would take me to the TD spread where I might find work. Someone shot me in the head when I was riding through the pass below that red mesa—'

'They call it Spanish Dome,' said Gabriel helpfully but Brett gave no sign he had heard.

'I guess I rowelled the buckskin. Next I know I'm in the river, half-drowning, with the reins wrapped around my wrist.' He paused and then shook his head slowly. 'Then I recall I was lying on some rocks with birds singing in the trees and Tess Dalton leaning over me – which about brings me up to date.' He glanced at the sheriff. 'Like it or not.'

All three seemed disappointed but Brett nodded, grabbed his hat and started out while Heffernan was demanding Wise hand over his notebook.

He went to the infirmary and was surprised to find Kip Benbow waiting there, smoking. Heffernan had forbidden him to attend the hypnosis session and the man had been bitter about it. After all, Al had been his brother and he had a right to know what happened to him – or what this Brett said had happened to him. . . .

He stood up now, Lacy's injured cowboy still sleeping in the next bed, snoring intermittently.

Benbow held up a hand. 'I listened in at the door. I had a *right*!'

Brett nodded. 'I guess – and what I said was gospel.'

Benbow sighed. 'Yeah, well, I know Al set out to get you and take you in for the reward, but my deadline to pay back the five hundred came and went and I figured you must've killed him or somethin' so I came lookin'. . . . He always hated snakes. Don't like to think of him goin' that way.'

'Wasn't pretty. Look, I think I can find the place I buried him, covered him with rocks mainly. The snakebite's the only injury you'll find on him.'

Brett said this, eyes steady on Benbow's face. The man nodded slowly. 'Dunno why, but I believe you.' He smiled ruefully. 'Mebbe *I* better take you in. That gambler'll come after me for his money.'

Brett stepped back a little, hands out from his side. 'Welcome to try.'

There was a hesitation but then Benbow shook his head. 'I don't think so. What you gonna do now? Go after the feller who shot you?'

'Didn't get much of a look at him. Pretty big, think there was long hair showing under his hat, but that's about it. . . . How about you? Riding on?'

'No, think I'll hang around a little. Dunno why,

but there's somethin' here that don't sit right with me.'

Brett shrugged. 'Well, I'm turning in.'

'I'll sleep in the livery's hay loft if the hostler'll let me.' Benbow went out and Brett stretched out on the bed, saw Chick Rendell looking at him.

'We disturb you?'

'Not really. I ain't been sleepin' much.'

'Must be mighty sore. Feeling any better?'

'Tolerably. Gonna ride out soon as I can.'

'Best thing. You get a look at the men who beat you?'

'Not really, but I been thinkin' about it. Someone called another feller Jethro and I'm pretty certain it was Caine's voice said to kick us till he told 'em to stop.'

Brett sat up. 'Jethro? That'd be Jethro Caine, Granger's hardcase?'

'Yeah – long-haired son of a bitch has been cock of this dung heap for years! Time someone put a bullet in him. No one ever beat him with fists. Or ever will, I reckon.'

'Long-haired, you say? Big man?'

'Bigger'n you. Not taller but beefier. He's a mean bastard – they say he's killed a couple men. Likes to shoot 'em from ambush. If he's facin' a man he'd rather kick his teeth in than try for a gun.'

'Sounds mean,' Brett acknowledged slowly, lying down again. 'See you in the morning, Chick. Pleasant dreams.'

'Yeah – I'll dream about a gal I know in Santa Fe, a long ways from here!'

*

Brett only slept for a couple of hours and then got quietly out of bed and left the infirmary. Chick Rendell was moaning in his sleep and restless but he didn't waken.

Brett made his way to the livery and didn't disturb the sleeping hostler as he saddled the buckskin in its stall and led it out through the double doors. The stars still blazed in the sky but the moon was spilling moondust from its sickle shape just above the distant Continental Divide. The town was mostly asleep except for a drunken duo singing a range ditty on the balcony of the whorehouse. Lights burned in the downstairs section and the saloon appeared to be still open. But no one else saw him leave town.

He felt tired but his mind was clearer than it had been for what seemed like a long time. All kinds of memories were stirring, making him restless. He skirted the law office by the back streets: Heffernan wanted him behind bars and Brett had no doubt that in the morning he would find some excuse to hold him here in town. He was just lucky the sheriff hadn't insisted on jailing him overnight.

So he cleared Lander in the cold dark hours of early morning and headed out along the trail to the Double L.

The same trail led to a fork a few miles out, one branch going to Granger's Circle G.

Brett hesitated, rolled a cigarette with one leg hooked over the saddlehorn and lit up before he made his decision.

He heeled the buckskin forward – along the trail to Granger's.

CHAPTER 11

EXPOSED

Hilton Granger hated for his sleep to be disturbed and had been known to gun whip a man who woke him before his accustomed rising time of 6.30 A.M.

That was why the cowboy who had ridden out from town, some redeye still swilling in his gut, dismounted by the corrals in the Circle G ranch yard and hurried to the bunkhouse. He wasn't drunk although his head buzzed a little from the rotgut and a night on the town. He stumbled going into the bunkhouse and a growling voice cursed him and someone threw a boot at him.

But he made his way to the corner where Jethro Caine had his bunk and his own small space in the bunkhouse. The cowboy's name was Colorado and he licked his lips before he reached out and shook Caine by one muscled shoulder. Colorado's heart was hammering his ribs – waking the tough ramrod could be almost as dangerous as disturbing Granger.

But Jethro came rolling over smoothly, the gun he kept under his pillow in his hand, ramming into the startled cowboy's midriff.

'It better be good or you're gonna have an extra navel, mister!'

Colorado swallowed and stepped back a pace. 'It's only me, Jethro – Colorado.'

'Well?'

'I just been in town, me and Dab Haynes.'

'Christ, I don't want to know what you two've been up to! *Why the hell did you wake me up?*'

He roared this last, disturbing at least half of the cowboys in the bunkhouse, but no one complained when they recognized Caine's angry voice.

'There – there was a fight in the whorehouse,' Colorado said swiftly. 'Dab got a bad cut over the eye so I took him to Doc Gabriel's.'

'Jesus Christ!' gritted Jethro impatiently, swinging his feet to the floor now and fisting up the front of Colorado's shirt. He rammed the gun barrel against the man's ear and cocked the hammer, feeling the cowboy sag as his legs turned to rubber. 'Ten seconds to finish or I blow your goddamn head off!'

Colorado's voice was high-pitched like a woman's now in his fear. 'Doc's wife wouldn't let us in. Said Doc was busy with that feller Benbow – only his name ain't Benbow, it's Jack Brett.'

Jethro stiffened and stared into the grey darkness of the bunkhouse, seeing the oblong of the open door.

'Brett!' he hissed.

He felt Colorado nod emphatically. 'Mrs Gabriel

fixed Dab's eye an'—'

'To hell with Dab's eye! What about Brett?'

'Well, I dunno. It's just that you told me the boss had been warned to expect someone called Brett but everyone reckoned he was that bounty hunter, Benbow. *He* claimed he'd lost his memory. Now seems his name really *is* Brett.'

'And maybe he never did lose his memory! Dammittohell!'

Jethro shoved the man away and the cowboy fumbled his way towards his bunk while Caine groped for his boots and shirt and hurried up to the ranch house, muttering.

Granger's reaction to being wakened was less drastic than Caine's had been but he was mighty annoyed and Jethro had to take a rough bawling-out before he could get in a word.

It stopped Granger in the middle of a fresh tirade. 'He's *Brett*?'

'Just like Blaine McCall said in his telegraph.'

Hilton Granger was suddenly quiet. Then, in the dim light, Caine saw his cold eyes glint.

'We can't take any chances. Hell, he could be on his way here right now – if he's only been fakin' that memory loss! *Son of a bitch!* Why the hell couldn't you've shot straighter!'

'I won't miss this time, boss, bet your life on it!'

'No, you're bettin' yours! Now get movin'. Take whoever you want, but make damn sure you kill Brett *dead!*'

Caine thought there wasn't any other way to *kill* anything, but he kept it to himself as he hurried out, deciding to take along Colorado and Dab Haynes. They had handled the beating of those two Double L cowpokes well enough. A little extra in the pay and they'd kill their own mother. . . .

Yeah, you're finished this time, Brett, or whatever your name is! You're dead – and just need buryin'.

'Which it'll be my pleasure to do,' Jethro Caine said aloud as he stomped into the bunkhouse, calling for Colorado. Haynes would be back soon and he might take that kid, Chuck – give the mean little sonuver some experience. . . .

Brett recalled having seen Jethro Caine briefly when he had gone to Granger's and asked for a job. He thought about the glimpse he had had of the bushwhacker after the bullet had burned across his temple.

Vision was wild, shot through with whirling bright lights, flickering slabs of darkness, everything distorted by the rapid motion of the buckskin as he fought to stay in the saddle.

Up on the rim – movement in the rocks – no more than a silhouette, battered hat, shoulder-length hair flying in the wind, settling for a second rifle shot. Then the world fell away under the horse's hoofs and they plunged into the river. . . .

Yeah, could've been Caine. He fitted the mould from what he'd picked up from the cowboys at Lacy's. Rough, tough. A bully and mean as a grizzly with piles. Granger's paid hardcase and troubleshooter. Heffernan said he was a killer.

Jack aimed to brace the man – and Granger, too.

That wire sent by Blaine McCall held new meaning for him now that bits and pieces of his memory were returning.

Wellington Wise might be a snake-oil man and a charlatan but he had called the shots correctly. He had said Brett would have flashes of memory now. Maybe not in correct sequence, but he would be able to put them in the right order with a little thought and patience.

There were many impressions swirling around inside his head – which still ached, maybe more-so than before the trance session. But he was getting back on the right trail now and knew what he had to do to stay alive.

First thing was to spike Jethro Caine's gun, then it would be time to square-up to Granger and get everything out in the open.

It was just coming on full daylight now and he figured he would arrive at Circle G in another hour or so. He wasn't too familiar with the trail, having approached the ranch that other time from over the range, coming in more from the south-west, rather than due south.

He was almost at a small knoll, dotted with boulders of sizes ranging from that of a chair to a small house. The buckskin was eating the distance easily, enjoying the cool air of the early morning. He let it have its head on the lope in to skirt the base of the knoll.

Then the guns opened up – a rapid, heavy volley that sent bullets buzzing around him like a swarm of hornets.

The buckskin swerved instinctively, hoofs driving through fountaining dirt. Brett hauled rein the other way and the horse protested with a rumbling snort but its big, muscled body reacted. As it cut to the other side, Brett slid his rifle out of leather, crouched low, legs like springs in the stirrups as he raced the horse for shelter.

He glanced up at the boulders above, swore softly when he saw three different guns spurting ribbons of flame-laced smoke. *Three!* They really figured to stop him this time!

Not if he could help it.

He rode the buckskin in amongst some high rocks, giving the horse as much protection as possible, before quitting the saddle. Brett dived for the ground as lead ricocheted with deadly snarls from the rocks. He hit hard and grunted aloud as the jar sent knifing pain through his skull. He pushed back his hat with a sweeping motion, rolled on to his belly, scrabbled in closer and rose to one knee.

The man directly above him was foolish enough to lean out for a better shot – and it was the last move he made – except to rear up and come plunging down through space, limp arms and legs waving, before he smashed into the rocks with a heavy, pulpy sound.

By the time the man had struck, Brett had moved away to another boulder, slammed his shoulder against it as he crouched, spotted a second gunman and levered off two fast shots. The man ducked quickly. Brett didn't think he had hit him.

The third man put a bullet within inches of Brett's

face, the lead fanning one ear before splattering against the rock. Bits of hot, shattering lead stung his cheek and he felt little warm beads of blood in several places.

He rolled away from the sheltering boulder and the second man appeared again, getting the best view. He levered and got off three fast shots. They hammered around Brett who rolled under a rock, one arm covering his head.

That had been close – too damn close!

He was breathing hard now, still couldn't get a clear shot at either of the remaining bushwhackers. They were holding fire for the moment, too, maybe moving to better positions. He needed to move from here. He looked around swiftly, decided where to go, but, just as he prepared to make his lunging run, one of the killers put a bullet between his feet. Brett stumbled and went down to one knee. The man above, elated, exposed himself on a flat rock. He was so clear, Brett could see the flash of his teeth as he smiled in triumph.

Then Brett, sliding on his back still, brought his rifle around and levered and triggered in a hammering volley until the magazine was empty.

By that time, the killer up there was no more than a pile of bloody rags huddled at the edge of the flat rock.

But where was the last man? Where did he go?

Brett started to reload and his hat was whipped off his head and he had the answer: the last killer was behind and above him! *And, goddamnit, he was trying for another head-shot!*

'Not this time!' Brett gritted, and screwed his body around, shooting the rifle wild, one-handed, just to make the man keep his head down. Then he launched himself into a cavity between the rocks but he no sooner landed than the rifle up there crashed again in two fast shots and bullets whizzed from one side of the crevice to the other, lead slicing through Brett's jacket: it was that close.

He was jammed now, his rifle arm under his body. He had landed so heavily that his weight had crushed him against the rock and he was going to have to fight to free himself. Brett started wrenching and twisting, his rifle actually a hindrance so that he was forced to release his grip on it, try to use his hand to thrust him up and out. It was a tight squeeze and every second he expected to feel the slamming finality of a bullet in the back.

Sweat poured from him. His jacket tore. He felt the knee of his denim trousers rip across. His boot toes scrabbled on loose gravel, unable to get a proper grip. Then, with a mighty heave, thrusting violently with the hand beneath his body, he tore free, snatched at his rifle and missed, even as he rolled on to one side. He was reaching for the Winchester again when he heard a rifle's lever clash only feet away.

Brett froze, twisted his head awkwardly, and looked up at a tall man with wide shoulders, greasy hair blowing a little in the breeze, stained teeth bared in a cold grin.

'I'll make damn good and sure of you this time, Brett!' said Jethro Caine, sounding pleased with himself. His finger started to tighten on the trigger, then eased off slightly. 'Is that your real name?'

Brett didn't answer and Caine shrugged.

'Hell, it don't matter. Be glad to put it or any other name you like on your headstone. So long, feller!'

There was nowhere for Brett to go. He couldn't throw himself in any direction. He was sprawled out in the crevice – and all he could do was wait for the bullet to slam into him.

He closed his eyes, jumped when he heard the whip-crack of the rifle.

Nothing slammed into his body and he opened his eyes.

Jethro had lifted to his toes and only now did his rifle fire. But it was a wild shot and jumped from his hand as another whip-crack sounded across the knoll and Jethro was hurled sideways, his head wrenching around violently. He spun, crashed into a boulder and spilled on to the rocks not a yard from where Brett lay.

Jack Brett wasted no time in getting himself out of the crevice, reaching for his own rifle. He heard gravel crunch under boots, looked up and saw a tall, lean shape silhouetted against the sky. His left arm came up and blotted out the sun and his jaw sagged.

It was Kip Benbow. And he had a smoking rifle in his hands as he came slowly towards Brett, keeping his gun pointed at him.

'I don't sleep as soundly as the hostler,' Benbow said. 'Seen you saddlin' that buckskin and figured I'd follow, see what you was up to. Lucky for you I did, eh?'

'Damn lucky, Kip. Guess I'm beholden to you.'

'Well, when I collect the bounty on you, I'll call it all squared away,' Benbow said with a tight grin, the rifle still covering Brett.

'You're gonna try to claim it, eh?' Brett kept his hands out to his side, still holding his rifle.

'Thousand bucks'll come in handy. Five hundred of it will get that gambler off my neck.'

'Only thing is, you just might have trouble collecting.'

Benbow frowned, looked wary, moved the rifle a little.

'I'll shoot if you make any stupid move! I don't have to kill you – a bullet through the knee'd hold you, I reckon.'

'Reckon so – all right, you've got the drop on me.' Brett nodded at something beyond Benbow's left shoulder. 'But that feller on the flat rock is still moving. I'd like a word with him.'

Benbow grinned fiercely, shaking his head. 'I ain't gonna be stupid enough to look!'

'You don't have to. Just follow me.'

Brett started over the rocks and around where Benbow stood. The lanky man looked nonplussed, unsure just what to do as Brett clambered up towards the flat rock. Then he saw that Brett hadn't been trying to trick him.

The man up there had been badly shot up, but there was still some life left in him. He was even trying to claw up his rifle but it lay just beyond the reach of his fingertips.

Brett heaved up on to the flat rock and nudged

the rifle further out of reach with his boot. He knelt beside the man who had taken two bullets in the body and a third had burned a red-lined scar across one side of his face.

'I've seen you before,' Brett said, quietly. 'Riding for Circle G. Someone said they call you Colorado. Right?'

The wounded cowboy stared out of glazing, pain-filled eyes but nodded slightly.

'Granger send you and the others to bushwhack me?'

The man continued to stare and just as Brett started to ask his question again, he nodded.

'Why? Why does Granger want me dead?' No response, just that stare that was fading gradually. 'Second time he's sent Caine after me, isn't it?'

This time Colorado nodded.

'Why the hell is he after me?' Brett asked, but Benbow thought he sounded as if he already knew the answer, just wanted confirmation. When Colorado said nothing, Brett asked, 'And how come he was expecting me?'

Colorado turned his head slightly, apparently surprised by the question. 'Someone . . . sent . . . word . . . said to watch for a man . . . called . . . Brett. . . .'

'Who? Was it Blaine? And why did Granger panic?'

'Wastin' your time, *amigo*,' Kip Benbow said quietly. 'He's through.'

Colorado was still staring, but the eyes were blank now, glazed over with that dull look that only means one thing – absence of life. Brett sighed and stood up, still looking down at the dead man.

'Reckon you'll have to go ask this Granger himself why he wants you dead,' Benbow said.

'Reckon I will. . . .'

'But it'll have to wait. I'm takin' you back to Heffernan and he can lock you up while I put in my claim for that bounty on you.'

Brett shook his head slowly. 'You won't get it.'

'No? Dunno why you keep sayin' that—'

'Because I'm going to square up to Granger and get this thing settled.'

There was a finality in his tone that had Benbow running a tongue across his lips and shifting the grip on his rifle. 'You forget who's holdin' the gun, feller!'

'Don't matter. You'll have to shoot me to stop me.'

'Then I'll damn well shoot you!' The rifle moved threateningly. 'Told you, I don't have to kill you!'

'Or you could ride along – back me up.'

'Huh?'

'Kind of keep an eye on your . . . investment, you know what I mean?'

Benbow frowned deeper and then a touch of a smile twisted his lips. 'If that don't beat all! Man, I've knowed some rannies with hides thick as ironwood but you take the cake, mister!'

Brett spread his hands as well as he could in his position. 'Could make you richer than the bounty – Granger's s'posed to have plenty of money. Won't be no skin off my nose if you look in his safe and decide you like what you see. . . .'

That got Benbow's attention and his face showed plainly that he was thinking it over seriously.

Then a voice reached them from a little below where they were.

'That's very risky, not to mention against the law. Why don't you ride with us and maybe you'll find all the answers you're looking for?'

They both wheeled quickly.

Brett saw two riders at the edge of the tree line. One was a cowboy he thought he'd seen somewhere before.

The other was Tess Dalton.

CHAPTER 12

ANOTHER MYSTERY MAN

Brett vaguely recalled the cowboy who said his name was Rich Ritter. He told Brett he had helped load him into the buckboard when Tess had taken him in to Doc Gabriel after she had brought him in, wounded, from the range.

Jack had a dim memory of the anxious face bending over him, a face that seemed friendly enough but at the same time rugged with years of hard living – like every other cowboy he had known. There were no soft-looking cowboys, unless they were greenhorns, and nobody counted them until they had earned respect and a proper place in the brotherhood of the range.

But he couldn't recall anything else about the ranch, the TD. It was a small place – leastways, the house wasn't very big, a single narrow rectangle of logs with a shingle roof and riverstone fireplace and chimney at one end. The barn looked permanent with hand-split upright planks for walls and a steeply angled roof to cast off some of the heavy snows that plagued this country during winter. There was a root cellar, a bunkhouse that Brett reckoned would hold six men at a pinch. The corrals were heavy lodgepole pine and in good shape, and there was a canvas cover over the pump near the front door. He could see the corner of a roof of some stables out back and he guessed Tess Dalton was a woman who took good care of her horses during the cold weather.

All in all, the TD spread was one of the best examples he had seen of a small cattle ranch, the pastures themselves falling away in a gentle slope down to the distant serpent of the wide Wind River.

'Looks prosperous,' Brett said, speaking for the first time since, far back, when he had asked why she wanted him to ride with her and Tess had merely said to wait and see.

Kip Benbow had ridden along, sour and impatient, almost as if he was afraid he was going to lose Brett on this ride to the TD ranch.

'I make a good enough living,' Tess allowed.

'Going to be rich when the railroad comes?'

She looked at him soberly and gave a small shake of her head, the long hair moving about her shoulders. 'I don't think so. It looks as if the track will be laid mostly outside of my land, although it may cross the south-west corner and earn me a little compensation.'

Brett nodded. 'Where's the main line going to be then?'

'Depends on that mountain on the Lacy spread,'

she told him and he waited for her to explain. 'If they consider it safe enough to tunnel, the track will go through a good deal of Lacy's land, cross right over Granger's Circle D and stay this side of the river.'

'And if the tunnel's not feasible?'

She shrugged. 'They'll cut diagonally across the Lacys' to the river, build a bridge and swing right around our valley, and back to Lander, missing Granger almost completely.'

'You folk'll miss out on a lot of ready cash then.'

'As I said, the track will only infringe on my property a little even if they do tunnel.'

He was silent as they rode down the last of the slope and into the main ranch yard. 'It bother you?'

She didn't answer right away. In fact, they had reached the corral and she had dismounted and was loosening her horse's cinchstrap before she said, 'Not really – I came out here for peace and quiet. I'm doing well enough with my cattle and like the rest of Wind River County, I'll save a lot of money not having to drive my herds far to a railhead once they set up in Lander. Money doesn't mean that much to me. I'd rather have my peace and quiet and keep the style of life I've made for myself.'

He badly wanted to ask her why such a fine-looking woman wanted to settle way out here, away from the other spreads, furthest from town, without a man. But he held his curiosity in check, off-saddling the big buckskin and dropping the rig over the top rail of the corral.

'How do the rest of the valley people feel?' Brett asked finally.

'Naturally, they want the railroad, whether it crosses Lacy and Granger land or jumps the river without touching the cattle spreads – although there are a few smallholdings across there that would benefit by a bridge. Mostly, folk just want the railroad, whichever way it has to go.'

'And what's holding it up? The decision about the tunnel?'

'I think it could be that . . . Rich, take Mr Benbow into the bunkhouse and I'll send Cooky down with some coffee and biscuits. Jack, will you come with me?'

Benbow didn't like the separation, stood unmoving as Ritter asked him several times to come along to the bunkhouse. But Benbow narrowed his eyes, watching Brett follow the girl into the house.

It was dim and cool in the big log-walled room which was hung with Indian blankets and beadwork and a few pictures. There was a tintype on top of a polished upright piano in one corner and it showed a younger Tess Dalton holding a baby in her arms, standing beside a tall, smiling man with slicked-back hair and sideburns. He looked to be about thirty and seemed a little uncomfortable in the suit he wore with a four-in-hand string tie at the neck of his striped shirt.

'My husband – and daughter,' she said quietly, as he lifted the frame and turned the picture to the light for a better view.

He spoke gently. 'Where are they now?'

'Dead – both of them,' she told him in a firm voice, but he could hear the effort she made to keep it that way. 'They drowned crossing the Wind River when a water moccasin attacked one of the horses pulling the wagon. . . . It overturned. My husband apparently hit his head on a rock and, of course, our baby simply drowned. Hank lived a few hours after some of the other men in the wagon train pulled him out, but . . . He didn't know me. Something had happened to his brain after that blow on the head. He thought I was his mother . . . he died in my arms.'

Brett put the picture back silently and turned to her. 'This is where you were making for – the land you'd planned to build on when the accident happened?'

She nodded. Her eyes were moist but he could see she was determined not to cry in front of him. 'Hank was a meticulous man, a caring, gentle soul. I'm not sure he would have survived the frontier anyway, but – he'd drawn up plans for this ranch, how it was to be laid out, which buildings we would work on first. I followed those plans exactly.'

'Then the whole of TD is a kind of memorial to him?'

She looked at him closely. 'You're very perecep-tive, Jack. Yes, to Hank and Teresa. He insisted we call her that, after me. But she was to have her full name at all times, not the shortened version that I use.'

'You've done well, Tess – I'm sure Hank would be mighty proud of you.'

Her breasts heaved under the shirt which tightened as she sighed. 'I'm surprisingly happy here. Their grave is on a small knoll overlooking the ranch yard but I – I've made myself only visit it on birthdays and anniversaries.' She gave him the suggestion of a smile. 'I had to work hard not to become too maudlin. And that grave is on the south-west corner of my land. It's another reason I don't really care for the railroad, but if it has to cross my land in that place, then so be it.'

Brett nodded. 'And what did you want me to see?'

He figured she was quite in control, but he was a mite uncomfortable: it was time to change the subject. Now she gestured for him to follow her and they walked down a long narrow hall, doors opening off each side, and stopped before the last one. She rapped on the planks with her knuckles and asked softly, 'Can we come in?'

A male voice answered just as softly. 'Sure thing, Tess. Did you bring – ah!'

Brett stepped inside with Tess Dalton and saw the man propped up in the narrow bed against the rear wall. His head was bandaged and the leg outside of the blankets was encased in a plaster cast. There were crutches leaning against the wall and the man, smallish, balding, reached for a set of wire-framed spectacles and set them on, pushing them up his nose as he looked at Brett.

'Well, you've been a long time getting here, Jack,' he said, smiling.

Brett frowned and leaned forward to see better. Tess moved to a window and held the curtain aside so that sunlight flooded the room.

Brett grunted in shock. 'Ashley Church!'

The missing geologist thrust out his small, though roughened hand and Jack moved around the bed to grip with him. 'Hell, everyone thought you must be dead. And when Heffernan came back with your Appaloosa the other day, I figured they must be right.'

'Ash has been staying here with me for a couple of weeks now. No one knows about him except my own men who I trust, and Doc Gabriel who has paid a few clandestine visits.'

Jack Brett looked from the girl to Church. 'What the hell happened after you left for Lander? Your report never showed up and Randall sent me to find out what had happened – the investors are getting a mite edgy, want the first sod to be turned and the first track laid and so on. . . .'

Church was sober now, nodded. 'I'd received a couple of veiled hints that I could make some easy money if I gave a good report about the feasibility of tunnelling through that mountain – and more thinly veiled hints that if I *didn't* turn in a favourable report something unfortunate might happen to me.'

'Who threatened you?'

'Oh, I think it – no, I'm *sure* the threats came from Hilton Granger. Jethro Caine was the man who delivered them to me in a roundabout way. Too subtle for him to have worked out for himself, so I knew he was reciting everything by rote. Granger stands to gain the most from that tunnel, of course.'

'Not Greg Lacy?' Brett asked, surprised.

'No, Lacy'll get a nice compensation package if the tunnel goes ahead, but Granger owns the most land where the tracks will be laid after passing through the tunnel and he has plans, I believe, to build loading pens on his land. He'll allow other cowmen to use them, too, of course, but they will have to pay for the privilege.'

'Well, it's not far to drive into Lander if they don't

want to pay, is it?'

Church smiled. 'But then they have the expense of the drive and still have to pay loading rates. . . . No, I think Granger's idea was a good one and would've made him a steady income.'

'Would've? I guess the tunnel project is off then?'

'I'm afraid so. I'm not just a geologist, as you might recall, Jack, I'm a seismologist as well – which is why Randall gave me the job of checking that mountain.'

'What's wrong?'

'A line fault – millions of years old, but I doubt it would remain stable with all the blasting necessary to drive a tunnel through. Even if it did, I wouldn't be prepared to recommend it because the constant rumble and movement caused by the trains passing through might well nudge it into movement – oh, not for years, maybe, but suppose it collapsed when a full passenger train was halfway through?' Church shook his head vehemently, grimaced and put up one hand to the bandages. 'No responsible company would go ahead under such conditions.'

'I'll come back to that in a minute,' Brett said slowly. 'I heard that Granger offered Greg Lacy double the Land Agency's valuation of his land.'

'That's how badly he wants that tunnel to go through. Personally, I don't think he could come up with the money but I can't be sure about something like that.'

'What happened to your report?'

Church smiled. 'I sent a fake one through the mail, mostly indecipherable figures from seismic read-outs – and decided to carry the real report personally back to Randall.' He tapped his head briefly. 'Up here.' Then his smile faded. 'It was as well I did – the stage was robbed, the strongbox, which incidentallv contained little money, was taken – and so was the fake report.'

Tess Dalton said, 'You may not realize it, Jack, but Granger owns a lot of people and property in Lander – including the general store, which has the postal concession. He wouldn't risk taking the report out of the post office section right in the town, but it would-n't have been hard for him to set up a stage robbery.'

Brett nodded. 'We'd heard he had a lot of folk in his pocket. Matter of fact, Howie Heffernan was a bit of a question mark. Still is.'

Tess laughed. 'He's Hilton Granger's biggest stumbling block! Howie's his own man and is afraid of no one. Hilton tried several times to break his contract with the town council but they all backed Howie. He's a hard man and not really very nice, but he's certainly not Granger's man.'

'Good to know – But what happened to you, Ash?'

Church fidgeted a bit and Tess said she would go get some coffee. The geologist asked Brett to roll him a cigarette and Jack made two, lit both.

'I thought I was being smart – made that big deal with an Indian for the Appaloosa so I'd have an excuse to ride out of town without having to resort to the stage. But by then Granger had his hands on the fake reports.'

'Would he have known they were fake?'

Church shook his head. 'He wouldn't've been able to make head nor tail of them. Someone in the know would have picked up that some figures there could suggest that there is a fault line that makes the mountain unsuitable for tunnelling . . . but it was only meant to keep him occupied while I made my run on the quiet. As you know, I'm blessed with an excellent memory so I decided not to commit anything to paper.'

'And what happened?'

Ashley Church looked decidedly embarrassed. 'I suppose what it comes down to is – I wasn't as good a horseman as I thought. That Appaloosa had a mind of its own and it threw me! Up in those hills you can see from this window, I broke my leg and cracked my skull and a couple of ribs in the fall. Luckily the Appaloosa came across some of Tess's remuda and followed them into the ranch here. She saw my saddle was hanging upside down and came looking.'

'Just as well she played it close-mouthed then.'

'Oh, yes, indeed! Granger's men were here several times on transparent excuses, looking for me, but Tess and her men kept them away and never gave a hint that they had even seen me. But I think Granger believes I'm here. Especially since the Appaloosa broke out of the corral in a hidden canyon where Tess's men had been looking after him . . . and the sheriff found him.'

'Granger knows something's up,' Brett allowed. 'Sent Jethro Caine and a couple hardcases to bushwhack me.'

Church's face was pale now. 'Did you really lose your memory, Jack?'

'Yeah. Some snake-oil man Doc Gabriel knows

brought it back in part. So I can recall now that I'm working undercover for the Wind River and Prairie Railroad and that Randall's waiting for my report – not to mention yours on that tunnel.'

'You can only recall some things?'

Brett nodded, lips tight-drawn. 'Back as far as Randall giving me the job to come find you and your report. Before that—' He shrugged.

'You mean – your childhood? Parents and so on?'

'Nothing, Ash. Far as I'm concerned, my life started for me a few weeks ago when Randall called me into his office and told me he was sending me to Wyoming.'

They both jumped as there was a clatter and a crash, and Brett whirled, hand palming up his gun, crouching.

Tess stood in the doorway, the tray of coffee and hot biscuits and the cream jug she had been bringing now in a shattered mess on the floor at her feet. The hot coffee had spilled on to her trouser legs but if it had soaked through and burned her she was ignoring it. She stared at Jack Brett.

'My God! That's awful, Jack. It's just . . . awful!'

'Yes,' said Church slowly. 'It means, Jack, that you must even have forgotten you have a wife and family back in Denver!'

Brett looked – and felt – as if he had been hit by a train.

CHAPTER 13

HIS OWN MAN

Chuck Kerry was only a kid, but he was a vicious kid. In his late teens he had already killed three men and had run away from home when he was eleven after leaving his brutal father lying battered and bleeding with a pitchfork sticking out of his thigh in the old family barn.

Since that time, Chuck had gone from bad to vicious. He had been taken in by rough men on the wrong side of the law and they had shown him no kindness. It took him some time to learn that he had to fight back against the brutal treatment they dished out to him. There was one man, the leader's brother, not much older than Chuck, who delighted in bossing Chuck around, making him clean up after him and the others, occasionally giving him a kick in the ribs, or crushing out a burning cigarette end against his neck.

The boss had looked warningly at Chuck, plainly

saying, 'Don't get any ideas of squarin' things!'

But Chuck had plenty of ideas and he squared away with that little son of a bitch without the boss ever being able to prove a thing. In a whorehouse, Chuck learned from a drunken old harlot how to spike a man's drink with chloral hydrate – make a Mickey Finn as the whore called it. He got his hands on some of the knock-out drug and spiked his target's booze. When the man passed out, Chuck took him out of town and laid him across the rails – just before the next cattle train arrived.

Even the coyotes couldn't find enough for a decent meal and the boss wept, blaming himself for having introduced his young brother to hard drink.

Chuck rode out, making his own way by stealing horses and rolling drunks. He shot his first man from ambush when a local rancher offered him ten dollars to do it. Then, when the man refused to pay, he killed him, too. . . .

Eventually Chuck found his way to Wind River Valley and Hilt Granger. No one believed his wild stories of having killed men but he recognized in Jethro Caine a kindred spirit, the kind of hard hombre Chuck aspired to. Caine used him when he could and Jethro became a kind of hero to Chuck.

Like when Caine, Colorado and Dab Haynes had set out to bushwhack Jack Brett. The kid was desperate to show he could be trusted and Caine told him he could come hold the getaway mounts, but to stand-by in case he was needed.

But things didn't work out quite like Jethro had expected. Chuck Kerry had witnessed the whole thing – and its aftermath when Tess Dalton and that cowboy, Ritter, had turned up. Hidden amongst the rocks with the horses quietly browsing a patch of grass below, Chuck watched while Brett and Kip Benbow rode out with Tess towards her place.

He figured he had better ride back to Circle G and tell Granger but, as he mounted his shaggy-maned grulla, he saw the pair of big field-glasses hanging on the saddlehorn of Jethro's horse. He had coveted these for some time. Jethro wouldn't need them any more but now Chuck figured he could put them to some use.

Taking the glasses, he followed Tess and Brett and the others, holed-up amongst the brush on the hogback rise above the ranch and focused on Tess's ranch house. Nothing much was happening – Benbow seemed reluctant but eventually went to the bunkhouse with Ritter after Tess led Brett into the main building.

Chuck was growing impatient, searching for a way down to get closer, when he saw movement at a window near the back of the house. Quickly, he got the glasses up to his eyes and adjusted focus. It was Tess, opening some drapes to let sunlight flood into the room, which looked like a bedroom.

Yes – there was a bed behind her, Brett moving around it. Looked like he was shaking hands with someone in the bed, someone with a leg in plaster.

It was grey in the room and he had to adjust focus again. Then he saw the man sitting up in the bed adjusting his glasses and he turned and the sunlight washed over his face.

Chuck whistled softly through his gapped teeth, his hand shaking now. But even though the image trembled in the lenses' field of view, he still recognized the man in the bed. . . .

'I'm sure it was that feller who was takin' all the rock samples at the mountain on Lacy's land, boss – settin' them charges in holes in the ground and makin' notes while I watched him like you told me to do.'

Hilton Granger had risen from his chair now behind the desk, frowning at the kid. 'You mean Ashley Church?'

'Yeah, that's the feller – the one you and Jethro said you knew Tess Dalton was hidin' even though she told you she hadn't seen him.'

'So – broken leg, huh? That's what happened – he was throwed by that goddamn Appaloosa! And she took him in. . . .'

'Thought I better come tell you, boss, after Jethro and the others got killed.' The kid was smart enough to curry favour openly when the opportunity presented itself.

Grange snapped his hard gaze to him, smiled thinly. 'You did real good, Chuck. I gotta follow through on this quick, while Brett and Church are together. Go get the boys, bring 'em in from the range or wherever they are. We're ridin' and you're gonna get a chance to show me just how good you are at killin!'

Chuck grinned widely, showing his chipped and gapped teeth. His cat's eyes that men said always had a crazy look in them, seemed to glow.

'I'm your man, Mr Granger!'

*

Ashley Church told Brett that he had a wife, Rachel, and twin daughters, Esther and Ruth, three years old.

Brett felt really strange as he shook his head, aware that Tess was watching him closely. 'I can't remember 'em! Hell, this is worse than not knowing my own name!'

Tess poured him some brandy and handed it to him. His hand shook as he got it to his lips. 'I'm sure it will all come back to you, Jack,' she told him in a quiet, reassuring voice. 'Your memory has started again now. It's only a matter of time.'

'Hope you're right.' Brett rubbed at his temple, feeling the patch of tape still covering the wound. 'By God, I've really given Randall his money's worth on this assignment!'

'You're an undercover detective of some kind?' Tess asked. 'Working for the railroad?'

They were in the parlour now, Church having come in on his crutches. He was managing pretty good now although Tess told him he was being overconfident if he thought he would be able to ride a horse so soon. Kip Benbow had joined them and the look on his stubborn face told them he didn't aim to let Brett out of his sight again. He leaned forward in his chair, waiting for Jack's answer to Tess's question.

'Yeah. The railroad companies kind of pooled their resources, got this bureau of investigators together. A bunch of us work for whichever rail company needs us. We're under a chief named Josh Randall. He gives us our assignments.'

Tess nodded, still staring at him hard. 'But – you're labelled an outlaw. . . .'

'With a thousand-dollar bounty!' put in Benbow, tightly.

Brett smiled at him. 'You're out of luck, Kip. That was rigged, just to give me some authentic background. There was no robbery where I took important papers – that was just a reason for making the bounty payable only if I was brought in alive. But it gave me background to put me on the run so that when I showed up no one would figure I was connected with the railroad. Sorry. You're out of luck.'

Benbow's face was white, his nostrils flared. 'You killed two men comin' here! Men who tried to collect.'

'One – the first man in Colorado, was staged, to kind of consolidate what I was s'posed to be – an outlaw on the dodge. My gun was loaded with blanks and the doctor was a fake. The other feller – well, he was mean and aimed to kill my hoss . . . I figure he's not much loss.'

Tess straightened. 'You're a hard man, Jack!'

He said nothing to that, looked at his glass and she refilled it. He sipped. Benbow was fidgeting now.

'I dunno what I'm goin' to do if there really ain't any bounty. That damn gambler'll still want his money.'

'Maybe we can work something out, if you back me up.'

'You still goin' after Granger?'

'He's going to make trouble one way or another

for the railroad. It's my job to smooth the way.'

'Well, I still dunno as I believe you about the damn bounty but – I'll back you for five hundred bucks.'

'I should check with Randall, but there's no time before we tackle Granger so – OK. I give you my word.'

Benbow insisted that he shake hands and Brett did. Then Jack looked at Church.

'You better stay out of sight, Ash. Can't have anything happen to you with that information in your head.' He paused and added, 'Wish mine was as clear!'

'Don't worry Jack. When you see Rachel and the little girls again, it'll all come back,' Church assured him.

Tess could see that Brett wasn't convinced and she felt compassion for him.

Then Ritter yelled from the yard.

'Bunch of riders comin', Tess! An' the sun's flashin' from the guns in their hands!'

Granger and his men rode up to the edge of the yard down by the corrals. Some of the riders had broken away before this and were now getting in position behind the bunkhouse. There were only two cowboys in there who had been working in the barn greasing wheels on the buckboard when Ritter had spotted the raiders.

The remaining cowhand was out on the range, repairing the brush fence that the Appaloosa had broken through. He would hear the gunfire but even if he came running, there wouldn't be a lot he could do.

Granger had ten men all told and they were men who earned fighting wages every day of their working lives. There would be bonuses if – when – they took the TD.

Granger reined down beyond the barn but where he could see the house.

'Tess – I know you're hidin' Ashley Church in there! You been lyin' to me all this time, but I'll give you a chance: send Church out and we'll ride off. 'Course he'll have to come with us, but you'll be left alone.'

'What about me, Granger?' called Jack Brett.

'Brett? Well, you're a dead man whatever happens, *amigo*! Sorry, but that's the way it's gotta be. You must see that.'

'I'm just an outlaw on the dodge who got caught up in this.'

'Hogwash! I got friends in lots of places. You're a railroad man! I was warned you were comin'. Blaine McCall did his best, too, but you fooled me when you showed up fakin' that memory loss and callin' yourself Al Benbow.'

'Then let's get to it, Granger – you and me. Meet in the middle of the yard. One of your men calls the shots – one, two, three – or drop a hat. You choose.'

Granger laughed. 'With your reputation? The way you took care of Jethro? No deal, Brett!'

'Have it your way. . . .'

Brett's rifle suddenly appeared at the front window and fired instantly. Granger's horse went down under him. The rancher yelled as he was flung over the animal's neck and rolled in the dust. Two more rifle bullets fountained dust and gravel around his big body. He rolled in behind the water pump, heart hammering, mouth dry. *By hell, that Brett could shoot!*

It was the signal for Granger's men to scatter and those in place behind the bunkhouse to open up. They started shooting into the bunkhouse, holding the attention of the two cowboys in there so they couldn't catch the riders in a crossfire with the house.

Granger's men had quit saddles now and hunted cover and some were already shooting fast. Bullets pocked the logs of the house, chewing splinters and leaving pale ragged scars in the wood. Tess and Brett fired back and a sliver of wood torn from a corral pole ripped into the face of one of the Circle G men who howled and rolled, dropping his gun.

The others pressed their bodies flat to the ground, dirt erupting about them.

Granger, still panting and shaken from his fall, only had his six-gun as his rifle was still in the scabbard on his dead horse. He clutched the Colt firmly, peeking out warily, watching the house. *Only the two guns. Tess and Brett – no!* He thought this last as a rifle suddenly blasted from a side window and a bullet ripped through the canvas cover on the pump, struck metal with a deep, musical sound and ricocheted, spitting pieces of hot lead into his face. *That damn Benbow! He'd forgotten about him!*

Then a gun cracked from the roof of the house and he looked up in time to see Ritter up there behind the stone chimney. *Goddamn! This wasn't going to be as easy as he'd figured. . . .*

But Ritter was shooting at the men attacking the bunkhouse. *He must be able to see them from that height,* Granger supposed. He swore.

One of his men, a 'breed named Dakota, had a bottle of coal oil with rags stuffed into the neck. He had lit these and was raising up, arm back, ready to throw the fire bomb on to the bunkhouse. Ritter rose from his crouch behind the chimney's stone protection, concentrating, aiming his rifle at the 'breed.

Granger bit his lips and steadied his Colt in both hands, hammer cocked, squeezed off his shot just as Ritter fired. The rancher saw his lead spang against the riverstone and started to curse, but then it ricocheted into Ritter's back, sending the man crashing on his face against the steeply angled shingles. He started to slide towards the edge and Granger smiled – but it froze on his face as he heard a scream that chilled his blood. He whipped around, saw Dakota engulfed in flames, rolling frantically about on the ground. Apparently Ritter's shot had smashed the bottle and the oil had ignited, drenching the 'breed.

The two men with him were up and running so as to get clear of the flames. Dakota screamed on, still burning. There was a thud and Granger spun back and saw that Ritter had hit the porch roof and spilled off into the front yard. He wasn't moving but there was a large patch of blood on his shirt at the back.

'Good!' Granger gritted, then turned and yelled to the men behind the bunkhouse. 'Someone shut that 'breed up!'

There were two fast shots as one of the men shot Dakota and the man was suddenly silent and still – but he continued to burn. The two men ran from the stench and the guns in the bunkhouse opened up, cutting them both down.

Granger felt a lurch of nausea: if this kept up he was going to lose this fight!

The thought made him curse and renewed his resolve and he emptied his gun into the front door of the house.

While his attention had been elsewhere, he hadn't noticed that Brett had slid out of a window on the side opposite to where Granger crouched. The railroad man dropped to the ground and flung himself into a rolling ball as a gun smashed twice in quick succession and bullets drove into the dust around his moving body.

He came out of the roll on his shoulders, somersaulting, twisted and triggered his rifle. A man by the stables lurched and fell, dropping his gun. His legs kicked as he clawed at his midriff moaning in pain.

Keeping close against the logs of the house, Brett slid forward to the corner where he could see the corrals. Benbow shot a man but he wasn't badly hit – he dropped flat and still fired his rifle several times before wriggling in behind a post.

Then Brett froze as a thin voice snarled, 'So you're Jack Brett? You killed Jethro, you son of a bitch!'

Brett didn't know Chuck Kerry from the King of England, but he recognized a killer when he saw one. And Chuck was already bringing down the shotgun he held to nail Brett while he still sprawled on the ground. There was nothing Brett could do except make a try to save himself – and his choice was mighty limited: he was too close to the wall to manoeuvre easily and his rifle was between his body and the logs. So he released his hold on it, gripped his Colt's butt and fired through the bottom of his holster as Chuck pulled the trigger of the Greener.

The kid killer reared back and the shotgun barrel wavered and jumped madly as he loosened his grip. Buckshot raked the logs and stung Brett's left arm, more laid a welt across his face as he tipped on to his left side, got his smoking Colt free and put another bullet into the kid as he fell. The shotgun jumped three feet in the air as the second barrel exploded – but it fired directly into the ground at Chuck's feet and the kid was dead before he fell like a bundle of dirty laundry.

Brett's ears were ringing and he snatched up his rifle again seeing a man running from the corrals, making for his horse. Brett fired over his head to hurry him along. Two other men were already mounted and making a run for it. Frowning, he looked around for they were riding south, away from the TD, but also away from Circle G.

A small tight bunch of riders was coming in over the hogback rise and someone yelled, 'It's Heffernan and a posse!'

Granger's men broke from cover, heading for their horses. Tess and Benbow kept shooting from the house and one man staggered, clutching at his arm. But Brett dropped to one knee, searching the ranch yard, for he hadn't recognized Granger amongst the fleeing riders.

Then he saw the man – just going in through the window of Ash Church's room.

Brett sprinted for the house as Tess opened the door and ran to help Ritter who was trying to crawl towards the steps.

'Granger's inside!' Brett said as he passed the girl, hurled himself through the doorway.

There was a gunshot and Kip Benbow staggered out of the hall, bloody hand pressing into his side as he stumbled and fell to the floor. Then Granger came, dragging Church, the geologist's teeth bared as he sobbed in pain with his broken leg thudding on the floor.

'Get back, Brett!' Granger snapped, smoking gun under one of Church's arm. 'Or I'll kill him!'

Brett stopped, eyes narrowing. He looked at Church's pain-contorted face and then at Granger's wild eyes.

'Hell, you're gonna kill him whatever happens. It's the only thing you can do now! So. . . .'

Tess, who had followed Brett inside, screamed as the man fired and Ashley Church jerked with the strike of the bullet. His dead weight pulled Granger off balance and the startled rancher let him fall, then started to bring up his gun as he was fully exposed.

Jack Brett shot him with his last two bullets and Hilton Granger was dead before he hit the blood-stained floorboards.

'My God, you killed Ash!' cried Tess, frozen with shock.

Brett knelt beside Church. 'Sorry, Ash. Hurt much?'

'Damn it, Jack! Why the hell did you have to shoot my good leg?'

Brett grinned, already tying his neckerchief around the bleeding wound. 'Had to make sure you dropped out of the line of fire.'

Tess stared. 'As I said before, Jack Brett, you're a hard man!'

Heffernan's face was stiff under its layer of dust. The cowhand building the brush fence in the hills had heard the shooting and while riding back, had spotted the dust of the sheriff's posse so rode to warn the lawman there was trouble at the ranch.

'Like ridin' into a goddamn war!' Heffernan gritted, glaring at Brett. 'I was right all along: you're one heap of trouble, Brett!'

'All in a good cause, Howie,' Tess said, still busy treating Church's new leg wound. 'There's really little for you to do here now.'

'Oh, is that so? You say that with a yard full of dead or wounded men, others still on the run – it might be some time before I can get the straight of this, but one thing I know I'm finished with right now.' He swung his rifle up and covered Brett, cocking the hammer. 'I've caught this one. And he's going in my jail till someone sends for him to put him on trial.'

They all looked startled, and Benbow, wounded and in a deal of pain, looked up as he pressed a bloody cloth against his side. 'Don't waste your time,

Sheriff. There ain't no bounty on him. It was all a set-up. He's a railroad detective.'

Heffernan snapped his head around, frowning. 'What's this latest hogwash you're tryin' to put over, Brett! I found a dodger on you – thousand dollars bounty for your capture *alive*! I'll get a wire off to Denver tonight and you can set in one of my cells until someone comes for you.'

'No, Howie,' spoke up Tess. 'He really does work for the railroad. The bounty and the dodger were just to give him a background so no one would suspect he was really a railroad man.'

'It's true, Sheriff,' said Church. 'I can vouch for that.'

Heffernan was quiet for a long time. Then he shook his head. 'If you can show me that in writin' – well, OK, I guess I'll believe you.'

'Well, I don't have it in *writing*,' said Church slowly.

The rifle jerked at Brett. 'Lift your hands – I'm takin' you in.'

'For crying out loud!' Brett gritted. 'I work for a man named Josh Randall in Denver. He's head of the Railroad Investigation Bureau and—'

'Then looks like he's the man I better send my wire to – and see if he backs up your story.'

'Christ! Of course he will! No need to hold me in jail.'

'That's where you're gonna stay till I'm satisfied, mister. Now, turn around and put your hands behind your back!' snapped the unbending sheriff.

He was holding a set of handcuffs in one hand, the jaws open. He prodded Brett hard with the rifle barrel and Jack sighed, did as he was ordered and looked at Tess, as the cuffs snapped closed.

'You were right – he's not a very nice man! But if you care to stop your ears, I'll tell these other fellers *exactly* what he is!'